THE CLUE IN
THE COBWEB

Books by

CAROLYN KEENE

Nancy Drew Mystery Stories

Dana Girls Mystery Stories

"Perhaps Uncle Ned would know who she is," Jean
exclaimed

The Clue in the Cobweb

The DANA GIRLS Mystery Stories

THE CLUE IN THE COBWEB

By

CAROLYN KEENE

Grosset & Dunlap, *Publishers*
NEW YORK

CONTENTS

THE CLUE IN
THE COBWEB

CHAPTER I

JEAN'S INVENTION

"JEAN, you've been playing with that old machine for over an hour. When are you going to study? Time's almost up."

The Dana sisters, Louise and Jean, were alone in their rooms at Starhurst School for Girls. During the entire study period, Jean, the younger, fair-haired one, had been absorbed in a queer-looking contraption she was trying to build.

"Oh, one may always study," she laughed in reply to her sister's question. "This invention of mine is too important to wait."

"Invention!" exclaimed Louise, peering skeptically at the odd collection of springs, boxes, rollers and piano keys. "So that's what it is? I thought you were trying to build a piano!"

"Well, you might call it a sort of *super* piano," Jean laughed good-naturedly. "At least that is the general idea."

1

"You seem to enjoy difficult tasks."

"The idea came to me suddenly, Louise. I thought how wonderful it would be if Starhurst School had a little machine which would copy music."

"Yes, and another one to write our examinations for us and memorize French verbs!"

"All right, Louise, laugh if you like," said Jean with an injured air. "When this thing is perfected you may be surprised."

"I certainly shall be if *ever* it is perfected," chuckled Louise mischievously. "Just how is your wonderful machine supposed to work?"

"It's very simple. You roll a sheet of blank music score into the machine. Then you play a piece on the piano keyboard and the composition records itself in ink on the blank page. How does it sound to you?"

"A typical Dana idea!" exclaimed a voice from the doorway. "Perfectly crazy!"

Jean and Louise turned quickly to see Lettie Briggs standing there, her thin lips twisted into an insolent smile. Because this girl enjoyed bringing everyone trouble, she was very unpopular at school.

"Oh, hello," said Jean uncomfortably. She realized that Lettie probably had been listening to the conversation for some time.

"Let's see this remarkable invention of yours."

Boldly the Briggs girl walked into the room,

ignoring the fact that Jean was trying to hide
her invention by standing in front of it.

"It's nothing—nothing at all."

"Just what it looks like to me," agreed Lettie.
"How utterly silly to think that a machine could
record music!"

"Why is it silly?" demanded Louise, coming
swiftly to her sister's defense. "I suppose
when the first player piano was invented folks
called that impossible too?"

"Let's see it work," challenged Lettie in a
superior tone.

"I haven't finished it yet," replied Jean apologetically. "And please, Lettie, I wish you
wouldn't say anything about my machine to the
other students."

"An inventor shouldn't be ashamed of his
work," retorted the unpleasant girl with a quick
laugh which revealed she would lose no time in
telling the story. "Oh, by the way, you girls
are wanted on the telephone."

"Well, it's about time you told us!" exclaimed Louise, her dark eyes flashing.

Hurrying Lettie from the room, the Danas
ran to the end of the dormitory corridor where
there was an extension telephone. The call was
from their Aunt Harriet, with whom they lived
together with her brother, their Uncle Ned
Dana, captain of an ocean liner. Jean and
Louise were delighted to learn that both their
relatives planned to drive from their house in

Oak Falls to Penfield that day and wished to lunch with them.

"We'll meet you at the Beckworth Inn at one o'clock," promised Jean eagerly. "I know we can get permission."

Both Dana girls were highly excited at the prospect, for it was not often they saw their uncle. His duties as captain of the steamship *Balaska* kept him away from home much of the time.

"Now don't you dare tell Uncle Ned or Aunt Harriet about my invention," Jean warned her sister as they drew near the inn. "I've stood enough teasing for one day!"

Captain Dana and his sister, having arrived a few minutes ahead of the girls, were seated at a table by a window.

"Well, well," declared their uncle in his hearty voice, "seeing you girls again is just like taking a deep whiff of fresh salt air!"

"You're not looking as well as you should, Uncle Ned," declared Louise anxiously, as she slid into a chair which he offered. "You've been working too hard."

"Your uncle had a very trying voyage," said Aunt Harriet in her musical, low-pitched voice. "I thought it might do him good to drive over here today."

"What is wrong?" inquired Jean quickly. "Something happen?"

"You've not seen the papers?" asked Captain Dana.

Each girl shook her head. They realized from their uncle's serious tone that something had occurred which deeply disturbed him.

"During the voyage from England an attractive woman disappeared from the *Balaska*," explained Aunt Harriet, who could not wait for her brother to tell the story. "Naturally, reporters and steamship officials have interested themselves in the affair."

"Do you mean the woman was lost overboard?" questioned Jean in amazement.

"Reporters have hinted as much," said Captain Dana grimly. "But I swear it couldn't have happened. There were no storms, and a close watch was kept at all times."

"What do you think did occur, Uncle Ned?" inquired Louise, her eyes troubled.

"Hard to say. Miss Blore was a peculiar type. Somehow I figured she might make trouble for me before the voyage should end."

"Her name was Miss Blore?" repeated Jean thoughtfully.

"Yes, Katherine Blore. Very striking in appearance. Reddish hair, blue eyes, and an unusually white complexion. She dressed in the most expensive clothes of the latest styles."

"An adventuress?" questioned Louise.

"Well, I thought so at first. To protect my

passengers I made a point of trying to become acquainted with her during the voyage. However, I learned almost nothing about her affairs.''

"When did the young woman disappear?" Jean inquired, her interest steadily mounting.

"The day we docked in New York."

"What about her luggage, Uncle Ned?" Louise asked, intrigued by the narrative.

"It was found in her stateroom. She had three suitcases and a trunk, but they were practically empty. Everything pointed to the idea she had drowned, yet I feel certain she did not go overboard. But unless I can prove my case, there will be a bad storm brewing for Captain Dana.''

"I don't see how the steamship officials can blame you for the disappearance," protested Aunt Harriet. "It surely wasn't your fault.''

"No, but a drowning or a mysterious disappearance is bound to hurt the line. The point is —I feel sure Miss Blore is still alive.''

"Perhaps she had a particular reason for wishing to vanish," suggested Jean quietly.

"My own thought," nodded Captain Dana. "Miss Blore was careful to tell very little about herself. She did drop a hint that she had relatives living near Penfield. While the clue isn't enough to steer a course by, it's worth investigating.''

"Jean, do you remember that fine house on

Clague Road just south of the city?" Louise questioned suddenly. "Unless my memory plays me false the name David Blore is printed on the front gate!"

"That's so," agreed her sister.

"David Blore is the name the young woman gave me," declared Captain Dana, his face brightening. "If you girls will tell me how to get to the place I'll drive out there after lunch."

"We'll show you if you like," suggested Jean quickly.

Across the table Aunt Harriet smiled wisely, for she realized that the mysterious aspects of the case had intrigued her two nieces already. Although Captain Dana was deeply disturbed he pushed his own troubles into the background, and for the remainder of the meal became cheerful and entertaining. He related many amusing incidents which had occurred aboard the *Balaska* during its recent Atlantic crossing.

At last they all left the inn, and in the Dana car motored toward the David Blore estate. Although the girls did not know its exact location, they recalled the road, and were able to identify the large, rambling house as they approached it.

"Suppose Jean and I run up and ask if this is the right place," Louise offered, stepping from the car. "The name seems to have been removed from the gate."

Leaving their aunt and uncle to wait in the

car, the Dana girls went up the walk and rapped on the massive door. In a moment it was opened by a young Chinese servant whose carefully combed black hair shone like patent leather.

"I should like to speak to Mr. Blore, please," requested Louise politely.

"Master not here," answered the servant, bowing. "You come again tomollow, yes?"

"I am inquiring for my uncle," explained Louise. "I doubt that he will be in Penfield again."

"It really is very important," added Jean earnestly. "Captain Dana wishes to talk with Mr. Blore about a young woman who traveled on his ship—a Miss Katherine Blore."

Light suddenly broke through the oriental's mask-like face. The corners of his mouth turned up and his eyes twinkled.

"Missee Blore here," he announced cheerfully. "You talkee with her maybe?"

Louise and Jean exchanged quick, significant glances. To locate Katherine Blore would be a stroke of good fortune indeed. Were they able to prove that the young woman was alive, no possible blame could fall upon Captain Dana or his steamship line for her supposed death.

"Yes, by all means let us speak to her," replied Louise eagerly.

Leading the two girls through a long hallway with highly polished floors, the servant ushered them into a luxuriously furnished living room. While the Chinese went to call his mistress, Jean wandered slowly about, admiring the costly bric-a-brac. Soon the servant returned alone. "Velly solly," he said with a shrug. "Charlie Young make mistake-error. Missee see no one now."

"But it is very important," protested Louise, distressed. "Please return to Miss Blore and tell her that Captain Dana came all the way to Penfield to talk to her."

"Charlie Young go. But think it make no diffelence."

When the servant had gone, Louise turned nervously toward her sister who was staring at a picture on the piano.

"Oh, dear, I don't know what to do now, Jean. This young woman may not be the same Katherine Blore who sailed on Uncle Ned's ship. And if she refuses to see us, how shall we ever be sure?"

Jean indicated the photograph on the piano. Louise saw then that it was the likeness of a beautiful young woman.

"I am wondering if this may not be a picture of Katherine Blore," the younger girl said quietly. "Perhaps Uncle Ned would know."

"The very thing!" exclaimed Louise excitedly. "Let's take it out to the car and ask him! But we must hurry for Charlie Young may return any minute!"

The sisters glanced around quickly to **make** sure the servant was still upstairs.

"Let's run," urged Jean.

"That might arouse suspicion," replied Louise, so the Danas walked out quietly, but tensely.

CHAPTER II

A TELLTALE PHOTOGRAPH

ONE glance at the photograph assured Captain Dana that the young woman was the same person who had vanished from the *Balaska*.

"Aye, this is Katherine Blore beyond a doubt," he declared with satisfaction.

"Then your worries are practically at an end, Uncle Ned," laughed Jean, taking back the photograph. "Mr. Blore's servant tells us that Miss Blore is here."

"Well, that does set my mind at rest." Captain Dana drew a deep breath. "But how did she get off the boat without presenting her passport? I'll have a few questions to ask her!"

"She refuses to see anyone," declared Louise. "And Mr. Blore isn't at home."

"Miss Blore evidently does not understand that her offense is serious. It would be much wiser for her to talk with me than with government officials!"

"Perhaps you can induce her to be reasonable, Uncle Ned," replied Louise. "Jean and I are having no luck at all."

"I'll go with you," said Captain Dana, stepping down from the car.

The three returned to the house, where Jean

barely had time to replace the photograph on the piano before Charlie Young padded into the room. If he were surprised at seeing a third visitor he showed no sign.

"Missee Blore see no one today," he reported firmly. "She say tell young ladies she have hard pain-ache in head."

"Did you mention Captain Dana's name?" inquired Louise.

"Oh, yes, Missee. She say pain-ache much worsee then."

"I can well understand that," remarked Captain Dana dryly. "I could wait here until she changes her mind, but upon second thought I prefer to speak with Mr. Blore first. When will he be here?"

The Chinaman glanced at the clock and began counting the time on his fingers.

"Master gone one hour—two hour—three hour now. Charlie Young think maybe he come one more hour."

"I'll give him an hour and a half to be certain," responded Captain Dana. "Please tell your master to await me at four o'clock."

"Charlie Young tell master," the servant replied evenly, escorting the visitors to the door.

"Obviously Katherine Blore is afraid to see me," remarked Captain Dana as he walked with his nieces to the car.

"Will you have her arrested, Uncle Ned?" inquired Louise curiously.

"That depends entirely upon her attitude and what explanation she offers. At any rate it should be a simple matter to clear the steamship line of any responsibility for her disappearance."

Although Jean and Louise offered no response, they both wondered if their uncle might not be a trifle optimistic. From what he had told them of Katherine Blore, they knew that the young woman was a trouble-maker. Her refusal to submit to an interview suggested that she had no intention of cooperating with steamship officials.

The Dana girls thoroughly enjoyed a mystery, but not one at their Uncle Ned's expense. Orphans for many years, they had been very happy at Oak Falls. The household was a pleasant one, enlivened by the amusing mishaps of Cora Appel, a kind-hearted but slow-witted maid.

While attending school at Penfield, the Dana girls became interested in their first mystery, one which concerned the disappearance of a beautiful study lamp. Other adventures followed in quick succession, one at Lone Tree Cottage, another in a strange hermitage. Recently, while visiting an isolated region along the shores of Moon Lake, they had been privileged to delve into the mystery concerning a locked room.

In company with other students from Starhurst School for Girls, Jean and Louise had investigated a camp site which the headmistress, Mrs. Crandall, considered purchasing. The property with acres of shore land included an old country home, long deserted. There, after many mysterious happenings, the Dana girls stumbled upon a secret staircase which led them into adventure, and ultimately to the locked room and its treasure.

"Well, we shall have an hour and a half to spare," remarked Uncle Ned, glancing at his watch. "What do you say to attending a movie at Penfield?"

"I hear there is a good show at the Rialto," declared Jean eagerly.

As the party drove back to Penfield, Captain Dana called attention to the dark clouds which were gathering in the west.

"It's just as well we're steering for a snug harbor," he observed cheerfully. "If I read the signs, a bad storm is blowing up."

"Oh, dear, I hope not," said Aunt Harriet nervously.

Once in the theatre everyone forgot about the weather. A surprise awaited the group. When the main feature ended, the news reel flashed upon the screen. Jean and Louise straightened in their seats as they saw a large ocean-going vessel steam majestically into view.

"Why, Uncle Ned, that looks like your ship!" whispered Louise excitedly.

"Aye, it is the *Balaska* right enough," agreed Captain Dana calmly. "News photographers were thicker than flies where I docked. But I didn't suppose the releases would be out so soon."

In a moment more a close-up was shown of Captain Dana himself. Thoroughly at ease, he talked with reporters and steamship officials, giving a dignified report of Miss Blore's disappearance from the ship.

"I hated the publicity," the man muttered under his breath to his nieces. "No way to escape it, though."

"Why, Uncle Ned, you make a handsome movie star," chuckled Jean, thoroughly amused at his discomfiture.

"You certainly do," agreed Louise.

"I only hope that when the mystery of Miss Blore's disappearance is cleared up they give me as much publicity," growled Captain Dana.

Jean and Louise wished they might stay to see the news reel a second time, but the show was too long to permit it. In exactly an hour and twenty minutes they left the theatre.

"Oh, it's raining!" exclaimed Aunt Harriet in dismay. "My new hat will be ruined!"

"Now, you folks just wait here and I'll bring the car," offered Captain Dana. "No use for all of us to be drenched."

Leaving Aunt Harriet and the girls in front of the theatre, he made a dash through the rain to the nearby parking lot. A long while elapsed before the car drew up to the curb.

"Sorry to keep you waiting," the kindly man apologized, swinging open the door. "The spark plugs were damp. I had trouble getting her started."

"You're a sight, Ned," gasped Aunt Harriet as she noticed his damp, wrinkled clothes.

"I do look as if I'd been swabbing decks," Captain Dana admitted ruefully. "Well, it can't be helped."

As the car drove slowly through Penfield, Jean observed by her wrist watch that it was after four o'clock.

"We'll be late for the appointment," said her uncle, frowning. "I am sorry about that."

"This rain may have delayed Mr. Blore too," replied Aunt Harriet cheerfully. "At any rate don't try to hurry, Ned. The roads are slippery."

The sky had darkened so much that it was necessary to switch on the car headlights. Even then the bright beams scarcely made a pathway ahead. Rain fell in torrents.

"This is a real storm," said the girls' aunt.

As they came to a small hill, the machine began to labor. The engine coughed and sputtered.

"Those spark plugs must be wet again!" Uncle Ned muttered impatiently. "The wind is blowing rain under the hood."

Despite his efforts to keep the engine running it finally died completely. The car stopped at the side of the road.

"Now we're stalled for certain!" the captain exclaimed irritably. "I'll have to get out and try to wipe those plugs again."

"Oh, please stay in the auto, Ned," pleaded Aunt Harriet. "The rain won't last long, and you shouldn't soak your clothing. You might catch a bad cold."

"It does look as if the rain is slackening up," admitted Captain Dana gruffly. "But I dislike to be late for an appointment."

"Surely Mr. Blore couldn't expect you under such circumstances. Why, this is a dreadful storm."

"It isn't even a little squall, Harriet," laughed Captain Dana, his good humor restored. "Why, I've seen storms so bad one had to lash himself to the wheel to keep from being blown overboard. But an automobile isn't as dependable as a ship!"

For nearly half an hour they waited in the car. Gradually the storm abated until at last after many unsuccessful attempts Captain Dana was able to start the engine. It was nearly dark when they drove up to the Blore home.

Jean and Louise went with their uncle to the front door. They expected Charlie Young to admit them, but instead were greeted by a tall, dark-haired man of early middle age. His eyes were shrewd and calculating, his gaze somewhat insolent as he noted Captain Dana's crumpled clothes.

"Am I addressing Mr. Blore?" inquired the captain.

"Yes. Captain Dana, I assume? You are late."

"I regret having kept you waiting, but we were delayed by engine trouble."

When Mr. Blore made no reply, Uncle Ned introduced Jean and Louise whose presence was acknowledged by a mere inclination of the head.

"May we come in?" inquired Captain Dana a trifle impatiently.

"Oh, yes—yes." The man stepped aside, allowing them to enter the hallway. There he paused to inquire, "Why do you wish to see me?"

"It is in regard to a relative of yours, a Miss Katherine Blore. She traveled on my vessel, the *Balaska,* and I regret to say disappeared under peculiar circumstances. I understand from your servant that she is here."

"I know nothing of you, Captain Dana, or your ship," Mr. Blore returned coldly. "My daughter Katherine is here—yes."

"I should like to speak to her."

"Katherine is having her supper in the nursery at the moment. I do not wish to interrupt her."

"How old is your daughter, may I ask?" inquired Captain Dana in bewilderment.

"She will be seven in June."

"Seven! The Katherine Blore I seek must be nearly your own age."

"I know of no such person," said Mr. Blore blandly. "Obviously you have made a mistake. And now, I do not wish to hasten your departure, but I have a dinner engagement."

He steered Captain Dana gently toward the door.

"Just a minute," began the girls' uncle, but he was not allowed to finish.

With a smile and a bow Mr. Blore closed the door in the faces of his visitors.

CHAPTER III

TROUBLE WITH LETTIE

"WHY, the impudence of that fellow!" exclaimed Captain Dana wrathfully. "He can't do that to me! I'll have him thrown in irons!"

"You're not on the *Balaska* now, Uncle Ned," giggled Jean. "This is Mr. Blore's house, and if we try to get back into it he could have us arrested."

"Yes, you're right, of course," acknowledged her uncle, his anger fading. "The way to handle this is through the steamship line's detective."

"Then you believe that Katherine Blore is not his seven-year-old daughter?" inquired Louise curiously.

"No, he looked like a sharper to me. I've seen too many of his breed aboard the *Balaska* not to recognize one when I meet him."

"While you were talking with Mr. Blore, I glanced into the living room," Jean revealed quietly. "That photograph of Katherine Blore was missing from the piano."

"Someone must have been afraid we would see it," nodded Captain Dana grimly. "I'll send a wire to the company detective tonight!"

He turned to walk back to the car, but Jean detained him by placing a hand on his arm.

"Listen!" she said in a whisper.

From within the house came the sound of loud, angry voices. Mr. Blore was having an argument with his servant, Charlie Young. Their words carried to the three standing by the door.

"You'll get your wages all right," they heard the older man say irritably. "Haven't I told you that before?"

"Charlie Young think master make much talkee," was the even response. "Owe wages three months now. Money come or Charlie go!"

Captain Dana and the girls did not hear Mr. Blore's reply, for the pair evidently moved away from the door. After a moment the three callers returned to the car where Aunt Harriet was waiting patiently.

"It is getting late, Ned," she said anxiously. "We should take Jean and Louise back to Starhurst and then drive home."

"We'll get started right away," promised Captain Dana.

"Your interview was a failure?" questioned Aunt Harriet, observing his crestfallen appearance.

"The mystery hasn't been cleared up yet," he replied briefly. "But I think it will be soon."

The long absence of the Dana girls from the

dormitory had caused considerable comment among their classmates. Lingering near the front doorway when they entered was Lettie Briggs. Her pointed inquiry as to why they were detained was ignored by Jean and Louise who went directly to their rooms.

"Someone has been in this place while we've been away!" exclaimed Jean as they entered.

"What makes you think so?"

"Because my music machine has been tampered with! I left it covered and the cloth has been removed!"

"That's right, you did."

Jean rushed across the room and examined her invention.

"It's out of adjustment," she declared indignantly. "But I guess no real harm has been done."

"Considering that it wouldn't work in the first place, I fear you have no claim to damages," Louise said dryly.

"Well, it may work one of these days!" Jean retorted defensively. "Folks laughed at Thomas Edison too."

"I don't like the idea of just anyone feeling so free in our room," Louise said after a moment. "I wonder who came here while we were gone?"

"I can guess. Lettie Briggs!"

"I was thinking the same thing," admitted Louise.

Later in the evening Jean met Lettie face to face in the corridor and questioned her, but as she had expected, received no satisfaction. The Briggs girl denied that she had been near the Dana suite.

Jean might have believed her, had not something happened which tended to prove her denial false. Going down to the library for a book just before the nine-thirty closing hour, she came upon Lettie writing a letter. The girl quickly covered the paper with her hand, but not before Jean had observed the heading. The letter was addressed to the Patent Office at Washington, D. C.

"I feel certain now that Lettie was in our room," Jean reported indignantly when she returned to her sister. "She investigated my invention, and she may intend to claim it for herself!"

"That would be most dishonest!" exclaimed Louise quickly.

"I never heard of such a mean trick," added Evelyn Starr, a friend of the Dana girls who had come to study with them. "Something should be done about it."

"Why don't you apply for a patent yourself, Jean?" asked Louise thoughtfully.

"Yes, why don't you?" asked Evelyn.

"The machine isn't perfected yet. It might never work."

"Lettie must never be allowed to mail that

letter," announced Evelyn firmly. "I know how to stop her too!"

"How?" questioned Jean curiously.

"Just leave that to me."

Evelyn's plan was simple. After bidding good night to Louise and Jean she went to Mrs. Crandall, hinting at what she thought Lettie was trying to do. As a result the Briggs girl was called to the office and compelled to show the letter she had written.

"I can make nothing of this," declared the headmistress after she had read the communication. "You seem to be claiming that you have invented some sort of music machine, but you offer no evidence, not even a drawing. The place for such a letter is in the wastebasket."

"But Mrs. Crandall——"

"Allow me to suggest, Lettie, that you devote any spare time you may have to your French. Mademoiselle tells me you are in danger of failing."

"Yes, Mrs. Crandall," said the girl grimly.

The following day Lettie was sullen. She would not speak to Jean, assuming that the younger Dana girl had been the one who reported her to Miss Crandall.

"Oh, why must Lettie act so childish and spiteful?" Jean sighed to her sister. "I am afraid she may try to make trouble for me at the basketball game this afternoon."

The Starhurst girls were scheduled to play

a match with a group at Wellington, some distance from Penfield. Lettie had not won herself a regular position on the team, but would be taken along as a substitute.

"We'll keep close watch of her," promised Louise. "The game is an important one and we can't afford to have anything go wrong."

Despite Jean's misgivings, Lettie acquitted herself very well at the game. She showed scant pleasure, however, when the Dana girls, working together as forwards, made one basket after another. Although Starhurst School won an overwhelming victory, the Briggs girl was subdued and glum. During the ride back to Penfield in the bus she had little to say.

"I think Lettie hoped we would lose the game," Jean whispered to her sister. "She is such a strange girl."

Presently the bus drew near Penfield. As it stopped for a traffic light, Louise glanced out the window. Noticing a man who was hurrying across the street with a traveling bag, she straightened in her seat.

"Look, Jean!" she whispered, nudging her sister excitedly.

"Charlie Young! Where do you suppose he is going with that suitcase?"

"I wonder. I'll bet he could clear up all the mystery about Katherine Blore!"

"He's the one person who could tell us if she is a child or a grown woman!"

"Let's get off the bus, Louise, and try to stop him."

It did not occur to either girl that their actions had attracted the interest of Lettie Briggs. She watched them alight, then waiting until their backs were turned, she signaled the driver that she too wished to leave the conveyance. As the Danas followed the Chinese toward the railroad station, Lettie was close behind them.

"There's something mysterious afoot," the Briggs girl told herself grimly. "I mean to find out what it is. They'll keep no secret from me!"

CHAPTER IV

A CRY FOR HELP

UNAWARE that they were being followed, Jean and Louise sought to overtake Charlie Young. He walked so rapidly they did not catch up with him until he drew near the railroad station.

"Oh, Charlie Young!" called Louise urgently. "Please wait!"

The fellow turned his head quickly, his face mirroring fear. When he recognized the Dana girls he relaxed slightly and waited for them to approach.

"You call?" he inquired, setting down his heavy suitcase.

"Yes," answered Louise. Then, to make certain she was not mistaken in the man's identity, she added, "You are Mr. Blore's servant, are you not?"

"Charlie Young was servant. Mister Blore refuse pay, so Charlie go!"

"I don't blame you a bit," declared Louise, adopting a sympathetic tone. "Did you work for Mr. Blore very long?"

"Six months, Missee. When I take job he say to Charlie, 'You velly fine boy. I give you pay raise soon.' He make only talk. Charlie not even get regular wages-pay."

27

"I suppose the work wasn't easy, either," remarked Jean, trying to lead him to disclose more.

"Missee Katherine velly fussy," Charlie admitted with a deep sigh. "She want this and that all the time. Ring bell like fire engine and say, 'Charlie, you velly slow, velly lazy.' "

"Miss Katherine is a young lady, I assume," remarked Louise, watching the man closely. "A little older than ourselves, perhaps?"

"Missee Katherine never have thirty birthday again," said the servant with a shrug.

The girls were elated at this information, but they were careful not to disclose it. Already the man was regarding them shrewdly, wondering why they were asking so many questions.

"Why you stop Charlie?" he inquired suddenly.

"Because we thought you might be able to tell us how to reach Miss Blore," Jean answered quickly. "It is very important that we see her. She left my uncle's ship, the *Balaska*, without signing the proper papers."

"Charlie understand about proper papers," the fellow answered uneasily. "Uncle Sam say Chinaman show them or get out of country!"

It occurred to Jean and Louise that perhaps the fellow might have had difficulties of his own with immigration authorities. They promptly forgot the idea, for at the moment their sole interest was in Katherine Blore. Casual questions put to the servant brought out the information that the woman had returned to the home of her brother two days previously. No doubt she had been aboard the *Balaska,* for Charlie Young had heard her mention that the voyage had been very rough.

"Something go wrong on trip," the Chinaman told the girls. "Missee Katherine velly angly since she come back."

"Did your mistress bring any luggage with her?" asked Louise.

The servant did not answer, for he was staring across the street at a man loitering in the doorway of the railroad station. Following Charlie's terrified gaze, the Dana girls caught an impression of a tall figure, his felt hat pulled low over an angular, cruel face. He was smoking a cigar. Now he tossed it into the gutter and started toward the little group.

Charlie gave a choked cry. Without a word of explanation to Louise and Jean, he seized his suitcase and darted away. The man in the felt hat pursued him at a run.

Burdened with the heavy bag, Charlie could not hope to get away, but apparently he did not wish to abandon his burden. As he tried to dodge into an alley he was seized by his pursuer.

There was a brief and violent scuffle. Before the girls could go to Charlie's aid, he was overpowered. His assailant shoved him into a sedan which stood at the curb and drove away hastily.

"Quick, Jean!" cried Louise, her gaze on the retreating car. "Remember the license number!"

"JZ—4093—oh, I missed the last figure!"

"It was an eight," declared Louise excitedly. "Oh, where is a pencil and paper?"

Frantically she searched her pocketbook while Jean kept repeating the numbers aloud lest she become confused. At last Louise found a pencil, but for lack of paper wrote the license number on the starched cuff of her sister's dress.

"I am afraid something dreadful may happen to Charlie," she said anxiously.

"Shouldn't we notify the police?"

"Yes, at once."

Unaware that Lettie Briggs was watching from across the street, the girls hastened into the railroad station. Using the public telephone, they called headquarters, giving a complete report of the incident they had witnessed.

"We'll watch for the car," the authorities promised. "That kidnaping may mean the start of another Tong war."

"But the man who carried Charlie Young away wasn't a Chinaman," protested Louise quickly.

She gave a careful description of the assailant. Then, feeling that she had nothing more to add, turned away from the telephone.

"We ought to get back to Starhurst," declared Jean, glancing at the station clock. "If we are late for dinner it will mean awkward explanations."

"Yes," agreed Louise soberly, "it's just as well the other girls don't learn about this incident. Any publicity might hamper the work of the police."

They were fortunate enough to catch a bus within a few minutes, and arrived at the dormitory just as the dinner gong sounded.

"We'll not have time to change our clothes," said Louise regretfully. "I hope no one notices our mussed appearance."

The hope proved to be a vain one. At monthly intervals the girls rotated at their places in the dining room, and as chance would have it, the new arrangement brought both Dana girls to the table with Lettie.

"Oh, my, but you girls look hot and tired," she remarked sweetly, sliding into the chair opposite Jean. "Aren't you worn out from running so hard?"

"I don't know what you mean," returned Louise, slightly puzzled. "We've not been running."

Glancing down at her plate, she felt a flush spread over her cheeks. In place of the usual silverware, which had been removed, was a pair of chopsticks! A similar set had been placed beside Jean's plate.

"Since you girls show such a deep interest in Oriental pursuits, I thought you might appreciate these little souvenirs," remarked Lettie in a loud voice.

With a supreme effort the sisters kept their tempers under control, guessing instantly that Lettie had trailed them from the school bus.

"It really was terribly funny," the Briggs girl went on, speaking to the pupil on her right. "You would have died laughing! They ran after a Chinaman for six blocks, and then when they finally caught up with him he looked *so* bored. He stood it as long as he could and then he ran away."

"Where were you when all this happened, Lettie?" inquired Jean coldly.

"Oh, I just happened to be near."

"Are you certain you saw *exactly* what occurred?" inquired Louise significantly.

"Of course I did! The little Chinaman ran into an alley! You and Jean just stood and stared as if you couldn't believe anyone would run away from you."

The Danas exchanged glances and smiled in relief. Evidently Lettie had not seen the mysterious stranger fight with Charlie Young and drag him into the sedan.

"Why are you girls grinning so wisely?" the Briggs girl demanded in a suspicious tone.

"I am afraid you must learn the answer for yourself," returned Jean. "With your marvelous powers of observation you should have no difficulty!"

This time the laughter was at Lettie's expense, and was carried beyond the dinner hour, for Louise and Jean made a joke of eating with the chopsticks. At the end of the meal they carried away the souvenirs.

"Say, aren't you going to give those back?" Lettie demanded indignantly.

"Give them back?" echoed Louise mischievously. "Whoever heard of asking for the return of a gift?"

"Oh, you think you're very clever!" the other said angrily, turning away. "Keep the old chopsticks then! See if I care!"

When they were certain the spiteful girl was beyond hearing, the Danas placed a long distance telephone call to their uncle at Oak Falls. He was told everything they had learned from Charlie Young.

"Then the Katherine Blore who lives at Penfield must be the woman who was aboard my ship!" he replied in satisfaction. "I wish now I had waited in Penfield another day and tried to talk with her again."

"Jean and I will go out to the house if you wish," Louise offered eagerly.

"All right, you might try it," agreed the captain after a slight hesitation. "I'll write a note to Mrs. Crandall asking that she give you permission to be absent from school."

After their last class the next afternoon the girls slipped away from the dormitory without telling anyone except the headmistress where they were going. A bus carried them within a quarter of a mile of the Blore residence.

"I hope we'll not have made our trip for nothing," Jean remarked as they trudged along the road. "Do you suppose Miss Blore will talk to us?"

"We'll find some way to make her grant an interview. Evidently she doesn't realize the seriousness of what she has done."

Presently the girls entered the private grounds. There was no sign of activity about the place and the front blinds of the house were half-drawn.

"It looks as if everyone may have gone away," Jean remarked uneasily.

Although she rang the doorbell several times, no one responded. The girls then walked around to a side entrance and rapped loudly.

"I guess it's just no use," sighed Louise in disappointment. "We may as well leave. What a shame! We should have come sooner."

As she finished speaking, both were startled by a strange moaning sound within the house.

"What was that?" Jean asked, gripping her sister's hand.

The girls waited a moment for the cry to be repeated.

"Help! Help!" called a muffled voice. "Someone come! Please come!"

"That's strange," said Louise, puzzled.

"Who can it be?" asked Jean.

In a moment the cry for aid came again. This time the voice was much weaker.

CHAPTER V

A Deserted House

"Charlie Young may be a prisoner inside the house!" Louise exclaimed in alarm. "Come on, Jean, we must learn what is wrong!"

She tested the door only to find it locked. The two girls ran around to the front of the building but could not get in that way either.

"There's no time to waste," Jean declared, picking up a rock from the ground. "I'll smash the glass in the door."

A hard blow shattered the panel completely. Reaching her arm through the opening, she quickly unfastened the lock. Then the two girls rushed into the hallway and went directly to the living room. There they stopped short.

"Why Jean!" gasped Louise, staring blankly. "I didn't expect this!"

The room, so well furnished upon their previous visit, now was bare. Rugs, paintings, furniture, in fact nearly everything except the window draperies had disappeared.

"I wonder if the entire house has been stripped, Louise!"

The dining room likewise had been cleared of all its furnishings. Before the girls could in-

vestigate further they heard the same muffled
cry which had drawn their attention outside the
house.

"Help! Help!" called a feeble masculine
voice.

"That must be Charlie, Louise! He sounds
half smothered!"

"The cry came from upstairs!" Jean added,
starting toward the steps.

The repeated moans led the girls to an empty
bedroom on the second floor. As they cautiously
peered in they heard a scratching sound on the
door of the heavy oak closet.

"He must be in there!" cried Jean, darting
across the room and twisting the door knob.

"It's locked, Louise!"

Although both girls tugged with all their
strength they could not open the door, nor could
they shatter the heavy panel with their bodies.

"What shall we do?" asked Jean in despera-
tion. "If we call the police it will take so
long——"

She broke off in mid-sentence as both girls
were startled by the loud ringing of the front
doorbell.

"Now what?" asked Louise in a frightened
whisper.

She and Jean moved to the bedroom window
and looked down, but could not see the person
on the front porch. As the ring was repeated,
a voice strangely familiar boomed:

"Ahoy, there! Anyone home?"

"That sounds like Uncle Ned!" exclaimed Jean in astonishment.

"Yes, it does!"

Racing down the stairs two steps at a time the girls flung open the door.

"Uncle Ned!" cried Louise, giving her uncle a hug.

"What brought you here?" asked Jean after a hearty kiss.

"Well, when your telephone message came Aunt Harriet began to worry," explained Captain Dana apologetically. "She was afraid it might not be safe for you girls to come here alone. She kept at me until I promised to drive over."

"We're mighty glad you did, Uncle Ned," declared Louise quickly. "The house has been stripped, and someone is locked in an upstairs closet!"

"We think he must be Charlie Young," added Jean breathlessly.

"Where are the Blores?"

"We have no idea," replied Jean. "Louise and I arrived only a few minutes ago. We had to smash this glass in order to get in."

The girls led their uncle to the upstairs bedroom. Testing the strength of the closet door, he said crisply:

"We'll need a ram. I'll see what I can find in the cellar or outdoors."

The captain returned in a moment with a heavy timber which he had found in the basement. Louise and Jean took hold of it with him, preparatory to breaking down the door.

"Aim high on the panel," warned Uncle Ned. "Don't want to hurt anyone."

The three rammed the door with all their strength. At the second impact the panel splintered.

"Why, he's not Charlie Young after all!" cried Jean as she saw the figure which lay on the closet floor.

The prisoner was an elderly man with white hair and thin, gnarled hands. His face had so little color that for just an instant Louise thought he was unconscious. However, as Captain Dana lifted him from the floor he stirred, and mumbled gratefully:

"Someone came—at last."

Jean ran to get a glass of water, while Louise searched through several rooms for something on which to lay the man. At last she discovered a straight-back chair which had been overlooked when the house was stripped. Propping up the old man on it, they pressed water to his parched lips.

"Take me home," he mumbled, slowly regaining his faculties. "I want to go home."

"We'll be glad to do that," replied Captain Dana. "Just tell us who you are and where you live."

"My name is Asa Wharton. I stay at the Beckworth Inn."

"I know where it is," said Louise.

"We'll drive you there," Captain Dana promised. "But I am wondering if it might not be advisable for you to see a doctor?"

"Stuff and nonsense!" exclaimed the old man with reviving spirit. "All doctors are quacks! I'll have none of 'em!"

"As you wish, sir. Suppose you tell us how you came to be locked in the closet."

"That scoundrel, David Blore, locked me in! A neighbor sent word to me that Blore and his sister were moving out of the house. I came right over because I own this place and they owed me four months' rent."

"Oh, this house belongs to you?" inquired Jean in surprise, for the man's clothes did not indicate he had very much money.

"Certainly it does, and seven other properties as well. But being a landlord is no fun, I can tell you! I've met unpleasant renters before but none as bad as those Blores."

"Tell us what happened," urged Captain Dana in a quiet voice. "Maybe we can help you."

"When I arrived the folks had nearly everything loaded into a moving van. I told them they would have to pay the back rent or leave the furniture."

"Then what happened?" questioned Louise

eagerly as the old man paused to catch his breath.

"David Blore told me to come into the house and he would write a check for the amount he owed for the rent."

"A trick, I suppose," commented the girls' uncle.

"Yes, it was a trick. When he had me alone he struck me over the head and jammed me into the closet. The air was so close I scarcely could breathe. I must have fainted. When I came to I called as loudly as I could for help."

Captain Dana gazed thoughtfully at the old man. Although he did not say so, it occurred to him that undoubtedly Mr. Wharton had suffered a mild heart attack.

"We will take you to your hotel at once," he offered after a moment. "Just lean on my arm, sir. Louise, you walk on the other side of Mr. Wharton."

Supporting the victim as well as they could, they led him to the Dana car.

"I'll have the law on David Blore yet!" Mr. Wharton said bitterly, as they drove along. "He can't cheat me out of my rent and attack me without being made to pay!"

"Have you any idea where the man went with the furniture?" inquired Captain Dana, steering the car onto the main highway.

"No, they were careful not to give any hint. Did they cheat you too, Cap'n Dana?"

"Not exactly. You see Miss Katherine Blore sailed aboard my ship and embarrassed the steamship line by disappearing. Of course it gave the impression she had drowned."

"Katherine Blore is no more drowned than I am!"

"I agree with you heartily, Mr. Wharton. But to prove the fact may not be easy."

"Those folks are crooks, and no mistake."

"Have you any evidence?" questioned Captain Dana instantly.

"Nothing definite. They acted queer from the first. When they asked to rent my house I thought to myself, 'Asa Wharton, you are an old fool to let 'em have it,' but I did it anyhow! And now I wish I hadn't."

"Uncle Ned, do you suppose Miss Blore could have avoided the immigration authorities because she was trying to smuggle something ashore?" Jean inquired thoughtfully.

"Well, that is the obvious explanation."

"Could she have stowed away until after the passengers left the ship? Or possibly reached shore by swimming?"

"She might have been picked up by a boat according to a pre-arranged plan," Captain Dana admitted reflectively.

During the ride into Penfield Mr. Wharton told the Danas all he knew regarding David Blore and his sister. Aside from his suspicions there was very little indeed on which to base accusations. As they drew near the Beckworth Inn, the old man became strangely silent. Louise and Jean observed that their uncle gazed intently at him several times.

"How are you feeling, Mr. Wharton?" he inquired once.

"Quite all right," answered their passenger briefly.

When the party reached the inn, Captain Dana started to help the man from the car. Suddenly Mr. Wharton sagged against the cushions, clutching his chest.

"I—I can't get my breath," he gasped.

"Louise, run into the inn and bring the hotel doctor," ordered Captain Dana crisply. "I was afraid of this. Mr. Wharton is having another heart attack."

The physician was brought quickly and ordered Asa Wharton carried to his room and put to bed. Assured that the attack would not prove serious, the Danas did everything they could for the old man's comfort, then left.

"I do hope poor Mr. Wharton improves rapidly," Louise remarked as Uncle Ned drove the girls to their dormitory. "He is nice even if he is outspoken."

Upon arriving at Starhurst School, Jean urged her uncle to stay for a little while.

"I have something special to show you," she said coaxingly. "It is an invention!"

"Why, Jean Dana!" exclaimed Louise in an

offended tone. "You told me I shouldn't say a word about it!"

"I know, but I am in need of expert advice," laughed her sister.

"What have you invented?" inquired the captain with a broad smile. "Not a perpetual motion machine, I hope. You don't need one!"

"It's a music recording gadget," explained Louise. "There is nothing like it in captivity. Wait till you see it."

Somewhat to the surprise of both girls Uncle Ned did not laugh when he viewed the invention. He studied it for a long while, asking a number of questions. At last he said soberly:

"Your basic principle appears sound to me, Jean. You may have something worth while here."

"Oh, Uncle Ned, do you really think so?" His niece's eyes danced with pleasure. "Everyone has been teasing me about it, even Louise."

"I've never heard that the road to success was an easy one," commented Captain Dana with a twinkle. "You'll have to expect teasing and jealousy."

"I've been working on that machine until I am nearly ready to throw it out the window," Jean confessed with a sigh. "It seems to me it should work, but it just won't."

"Why not try using a heavier spring?" suggested her kindly relative thoughtfully. "You have no chance with such a light one. Now I must be going. Good luck to you with it, my dear.''

The girls escorted their uncle downstairs. As they passed through the lower front hall, Lettie Briggs, catching sight of Captain Dana, instantly recognized the man from Oak Falls.

"Good afternoon, Captain," she said in a shrill voice. "This is a surprise seeing you here."

"I just ran over for a little visit with my nieces," Uncle Ned replied politely.

He started to move on but Lettie had no intention of allowing him to pass. Aware that a number of students were loitering nearby she said in a gushing voice:

"I saw you in a news reel the other day, Captain Dana!"

"Indeed?" he inquired, shifting his weight uncomfortably. "That happens once in a while."

"Yes," went on Lettie, casting a malicious glance at Louise and Jean. "I surely was shocked to learn about that poor woman who jumped overboard! Tell me, Captain Dana, will they deprive you of your position because of it?"

CHAPTER VI

WHITE MICE

LETTIE's pointed remark was embarrassing to Captain Dana as well as to Louise and Jean. Before a reply could be made, Mrs. Crandall came into the hall and saw the visitor.

"Good afternoon, Captain Dana," she said cordially. "I couldn't help hearing what Lettie just said. Is it true that you are giving up your ship, the *Balaska?*"

"Not at all, not at all," responded the man gruffly. "The young lady seems to have gained a wrong impression."

The headmistress gazed sternly at Lettie, for she well knew the girl's habit of distorting facts and causing annoyance to others.

"I just asked Captain Dana if he *intended* to give up the ship," came the quick defense. "There's reason enough for him to do so, I guess!"

"Please explain your words, Lettie."

"Well, a young woman jumped overboard and drowned, didn't she? It was all in the news reel!"

"Even if these facts were true the steamship company would not request me to give up my

46

ship," said Captain Dana quietly. "Actually Miss Katherine Blore did not jump overboard. She did disappear from the vessel, but due to the clever assistance of my two nieces, I have traced her to Penfield."

"Lettie, you owe Captain Dana an apology," declared Mrs. Crandall sternly. "I can't understand why you would say such a thing!"

"I'm sorry," muttered Lettie, her gaze on the floor.

"And now please go to your room until dinner," the headmistress requested. "I consider it advisable for you to spend more time with your studies and less at the movies."

After Lettie had gone, Mrs. Crandall offered her own apology for the girl's actions. Captain Dana, with his usual good humor, made light of the affair.

"Now I must be driving back to Oak Falls," he declared, glancing at his watch. "I only wish my nieces were going with me."

"I wish we were too, Uncle Ned," said Jean wistfully.

"It could be arranged," offered the headmistress with only a slight hesitation. "You girls stand high in your classes. As a rule, I tend to frown upon week-end absences, but your cases are different."

"Oh, thank you, Mrs. Crandall," Louise murmured gratefully.

The girls hastened to their rooms to gather

together a few things which would be needed for the trip. In their haste they neglected to put away Jean's invention or to lock the door as they left.

Word spread rapidly through the dormitory that Louise and Jean had been granted week-end privileges. Ina Mason, a girl of weak character and sly ways, brought the news to her chum Lettie.

"Why, that is unfair!" exclaimed the latter indignantly. "Only this morning I asked Mrs. Crandall if I might go to visit my parents and she said I couldn't leave!"

"Mrs. Crandall always did favor the Dana girls. They make me sick."

"Yes, they are her pets all right, Ina."

"I think she should allow you to go home, Lettie. Why, your parents are wealthy and very influential!"

"Mrs. Crandall doesn't seem to realize that fact," Lettie responded with an angry toss of her head. "The idea of her telling me to stay in my room until dinner time—as if I were a child!"

"I shouldn't do it if I were you."

"No, I'll show her!" cried Lettie, springing to her feet. "I'll get even with Jean and Louise Dana, too!"

"What will you do?" asked Ina, beginning to get frightened, for she had been punished at times with Lettie.

"First I shall go to Penfield and buy something," was the response.

"If Mrs. Crandall should catch you——"

"She won't know about it unless you tell her, Ina Mason."

"Oh, I won't tell a soul."

"I don't trust you completely," Lettie said bluntly. "I'm not going to reveal my plan to anyone, and then I will be sure it will go off well."

Waiting until she was certain that Mrs. Crandall would not see her, Lettie slipped stealthily from the building. Taking a bus to Penfield she went directly to a pet store and bought two white mice which she carried back to the school in a shoe box.

Stealing quietly to the doorway of the Crandall suite, Lettie listened for a moment. Satisfied that the headmistress was not inside, she opened the door and let the white mice out of the box. They scampered across the floor, disappearing under the davenport.

"Mrs. Crandall will be frightened half out of her wits when they come from their hiding place!" Lettie told herself gleefully. "She is deathly afraid of rats and mice."

Softly closing the door again, Lettie tiptoed back to her own part of the dormitory. Passing the telephone booths at the end of the hallway, she noticed that Evelyn Starr was talking with someone. She paused to listen.

"Yes, Jean," she heard the girl say, "I will take care of it for you. Don't worry a bit about your invention. I'll lock the door immediately."

"So Jean Dana is afraid someone will hurt that silly old music machine!" Lettie told herself contemptuously. "If I were interested in looking at it I could get into her room all right!"

Although the girl had been in a very unpleasant mood, the thought of how Mrs. Crandall would react to the white mice revived her spirits. Returning to her room, she fortified herself with a novel and a box of forbidden candy, and left the door open so she would be sure to hear the first cry of alarm from the headmistress.

Unknown to Lettie, Mr. and Mrs. Crandall had returned to their suite. Finding the rooms somewhat stuffy they immediately had opened the door into the hall. Presently the mice scampered from their hiding place, and unnoticed by the couple, took refuge in the dark corridor.

When the gong sounded for dinner, Lettie went downstairs, leaving the door to her room open. The mice, attracted by the scent of candy, soon took up their quarters within.

During the early hours of the evening the girl read in bed, nibbled more chocolates, and finally fell asleep with the candy box still beside her. Just before midnight she suddenly awoke, aware that something had touched her hand. She heard a rustle of paper in the container.

"There's an animal in this bed!" the girl thought in terror.

When she switched on the light, she saw a pair of white mice flash across the quilt, run down a bed post and hide in a corner of the room.

"Help! Help!" shrieked Lettie, scrambling from beneath the blankets.

Seizing a book, she hurled it with full force at the mice. In her excitement she brushed a lamp from the table. It fell to the floor with a crash, awakening several students.

Next Lettie opened the door and tried to drive the mice into the hallway. Before she could succeed in her purpose several girls came running to inquire what was wrong. Lights were being snapped on throughout the building.

"Don't stand there and laugh!" cried Lettie furiously. "Do something! Help me get these mice out of my room before Mrs. Crandall comes up here!"

"She's coming now," chuckled Evelyn Starr, secretly gleeful of Lettie's worry.

Under the direction of the headmistress the mice finally were driven out of the dormitory. When the commotion died down Mrs. Crandall had many questions to ask.

"I tell you I don't know how the mice happened to be in my room," Lettie answered sullenly. "I just woke up and found them on my bed."

"I am not entirely satisfied with your explanation," returned the woman briefly. "However, for the time being we will speak no more about it."

After the headmistress had gone, Lettie slipped into Ina Mason's room which adjoined her own.

"I guess I fooled Mrs. Crandall that time," she declared joyfully. "She never dreamed the mice belonged to me."

"She may find out."

"Not unless you tell her, Ina Mason!"

"Oh, I won't tell."

"Well, I rather guess you better not," said Lettie with significant emphasis. She helped herself to Ina's bed, calmly pulling the covers up around her chin.

"Say, that's my bed," protested the other girl. "It's too narrow for both of us."

"Then you may sleep in my room," returned Lettie indifferently. "You won't catch me going back there!"

Lettie paid no attention to Ina's protests. Switching off the light, she settled herself for a comfortable sleep. In the morning the selfish girl half expected a call to the office. When none came she breathed a sigh of relief, deciding that Mrs. Crandall had forgotten about the white mice.

Her feeling of security was a false one. Directly after breakfast the headmistress drove to Penfield, presenting herself at the Jordan Pet Shop.

"Good morning, Ma'am," said the owner, who had never seen the woman before. "May I show you a nice pet?"

"I am interested in white mice," replied Mrs. Crandall, gazing about. "Have you any for sale?"

"Now isn't that too bad? I sold the last pair yesterday."

"Indeed?"

"Yes, to a girl from Starhurst School. She told me her parents are very wealthy."

"Perhaps she was Lettie Briggs."

"I believe Briggs was the name. She needed the mice so she could play a little joke on the headmistress. I am really sorry I haven't any more, but if you'll come in again next week——"

"It doesn't matter now," returned Mrs. Crandall. "In fact, I rather doubt that I should care to own a pair of white mice."

She smiled and turned away, leaving the owner of the pet shop to stare after her in bewilderment.

"Now what did she mean by that?" he muttered, scratching his head. "I wonder if maybe I told something I shouldn't!"

As Mrs. Crandall returned to Starhurst she

tried to decide what procedure she should take.

"So Lettie bought the mice to scare *me!*" she reflected. "And Fate turned the joke on her! That's almost enough punishment. However——"

CHAPTER VII

AN ALARMING DISAPPEARANCE

FAR removed from mice and mischief, Louise and Jean were spending an enjoyable week-end at Oak Falls.

"How good it seems to have you girls home again even for two days," declared Aunt Harriet happily.

"And it's good to be here, too," replied Jean warmly. "Has anything happened while we were away? Any births, deaths or marriages?"

"I've written you all the news. Oh, yes, Cora Appel has adopted a kitten. It came to the door last night and she didn't have the heart not to let it in."

"Well, that's nice," said Louise absently. "There's nothing cuter than a playful kitten."

"I am not sure how it will work out," sighed Aunt Harriet. "Cora is so interested in her 'baby,' as she calls it that she doesn't know what she is doing half the time."

"I never knew a time when she did," laughed Jean, lowering her voice.

The Dana sisters were very fond of "Apple-core" as they affectionately called the maid, but her awkward ways annoyed everyone at

55

times. Cora, however, was intensely loyal to the family and any mistakes were of the mind and not of the heart.

"Oh, dear, I do hope that girl will keep her wits about her today," remarked Aunt Harriet anxiously. "I am expecting a visitor."

"You didn't tell us that," said Louise in surprise.

"I thought I mentioned it. Mrs. Fred Mac-Vey is coming to see me."

"Didn't we meet her years ago?" inquired Jean thoughtfully. "An attractive woman with three children?"

"The number has increased to six. She and her husband have been living in the West. Now they plan to make their home in this state, near Penfield, I believe."

"Are they bringing all the children here today?" Louise asked, laughing.

"No, Mrs. MacVey is coming alone," smiled Aunt Harriet. "I haven't seen her in years, so I do hope the visit will go off well."

"Then I shouldn't trust Applecore too far," said Jean warningly. "With a kitten on her mind, you can't tell what might happen."

"I made the dessert myself last evening. A delicious chocolate ice box cake. Cora should be able to serve it——"

Aunt Harriet's words trailed away as a loud crash came from the kitchen.

"Now what?" she gasped in dismay. "If

Cora has dropped my ice box dessert, I shall never forgive her!"

Fearing the worst, the three hastened to the kitchen. Aunt Harriet's dessert was undamaged, but on the floor lay a broken bottle of milk which had fallen from the table. While the maid stood by, helplessly wringing her hands, the kitten began to lap up the liquid.

"Oh, Miss Dana," the girl moaned. "I don't know how it happened, I don't. I was polishin' the silver coffee pot like you told me to do, when I heard an awful crash! My baby must have done it."

"Cora, didn't I ask you to keep your pet in the basement?" asked Aunt Harriet severely.

"Yes'm, and I been keepin' her there. Only sometimes the door into the cellar comes open, and the little thing gets into the kitchen. I put her down every time she jumps on the table, but seems like it don't do no good."

"Well, clean up the mess," sighed Aunt Harriet, turning away. "And try to think what you are doing today. Mrs. MacVey will arrive at three o'clock."

"She'll be here before I know it," agreed the maid in a nervous flutter. "There's the dustin' to do, and the lunch dishes ain't out of the way yet. Seems like everything goes wrong when I'm busy."

The Dana girls felt sorry for her.

"We'll help you with the dishes, Cora," offered Louise. "But first let's clean up the milk and put the kitten into the basement again."

Long before three o'clock everything was in readiness for Mrs. MacVey's call. Aunt Harriet told Cora exactly how to serve the tea, repeating the instructions several times.

"I don't see how she can possibly mix up my orders," the woman sighed, "but I have a feeling something will go wrong."

Jean and Louise found the caller a very entertaining woman. Besides having an interesting personality, she told intriguing tales of the West. She mentioned too the lively ways of her six children.

"So far I haven't been able to find a house large enough for my brood," she laughed lightly. "We need a regular farm, you know."

It occurred to the girls that the visitor might be interested in Mr. Wharton's house, left empty by the sudden departure of the Blore family. After listening to their description of it, Mrs. MacVey declared that the place appeared to be just what she wanted.

"I hope the rent isn't too high," she remarked anxiously. "With six children to provide for, my husband and I can't afford anything extravagant."

"I have no idea how much Mr. Wharton is asking," Louise told her. "If you wish, Jean and I will inquire of him when we return to Penfield."

"Oh, I wish you would," the woman said gratefully. "We must find a house soon."

The afternoon passed pleasantly. Soon the time for refreshments drew near. When Applecore did not appear, Jean and Louise went quietly to the kitchen to see what was the matter. The maid was not in sight.

"Now what can have become of her?" Louise asked, annoyed.

"We'll have to serve tea ourselves, I guess," added Jean.

The girl went to the ice box for the dessert which her aunt had prepared. As she opened the door out leaped the kitten, its paws covered with chocolate!

The sisters were so stunned they could not say a word. Somehow the pet had managed to get into the refrigerator. Cora in her stupid way probably had slammed the door shut. Now Miss Dana's ice box cake, and for that matter everything else in the refrigerator, was a wreck!

"I never saw a worse mess!" said Louise.

"This will break Aunt Harriet's heart," murmured Jean at last. "What shall we do?"

While they were gloomily surveying the wreckage the maid came into the kitchen from out-of-doors.

"Oh, Applecore, where have you been?" Louise cried accusingly. "Such a mess as we are in now!"

"I just went down to the store," replied the girl. "Is it time to serve the chocolate dessert and put the kettle on for tea?"

"It's past time," replied Jean severely. "Just see what has happened! Have you any idea how your kitten got into the ice box?"

"Oh, ain't that just awful?" moaned the maid as she saw the damage which had been done. "I dunno how my baby ever jumped in there. Now what will Miss Dana say?"

"Do you remember leaving the ice box door open, Cora?" questioned Louise.

"Maybe I did just for a little bit, but I closed it tight again."

"And locked the kitten inside," Louise added in a resigned tone. "Well, it's too late to do anything about it now."

"Poor kitty," was the girl's only comment.

"Cora, is that a container of ice cream you have?" Jean demanded suddenly.

"Yes'm, your Aunt Harriet said she wanted some for supper——"

The girls waited to hear no more. Seizing the carton they quickly estimated its contents.

"If we give ourselves very small portions it should go around," Louise declared. "We'll save the day yet! Hurry, Cora, and put the water on to boil."

"I'm so flustered I dunno which way to turn. I've plumb forgot everything your Aunt Harriet said I was to do."

"Never mind," said Jean quickly, "I'll attend to the kettle. Just take your kitten into the basement and wipe the food off her."

A few minutes later the girls carried the refreshments to the living room. A startled expression passed over Aunt Harriet's face, but she ate her portion of ice cream without comment. The caller seemed to notice nothing amiss; in fact, she was complimentary about the food. Not until Mrs. MacVey had departed did the girls have an opportunity to explain what had happened.

All too soon Louise and Jean found that it was time to return to Penfield. They had related their meeting with Charlie Young, and both Uncle Ned and Aunt Harriet expressed deep concern for the Oriental's safety. Before leaving for Penfield the girls gave their aunt a copy of the license number which they had noted down. She promised to call the police at once if ever she should see a car bearing the same number.

At Starhurst School once more, the sisters learned the details of the misadventure of Lettie Briggs with the white mice. As a result of the prank, her social privileges had been withdrawn for a month.

The Dana girls did not forget their promise to Mrs. MacVey. At the first opportunity they called on Mr. Wharton, finding him greatly improved in health. Since the doctor had ordered his patient not to leave his bed, he asked Louise and Jean if they would mind showing the house to their friend.

"We'd love to do it," offered the older girl promptly.

Mr. Wharton gave them the key and the following day they met Mrs. MacVey on the premises.

"I like the outside of the house," the woman declared as they entered. "The spacious grounds will be wonderful for my boys. Did Mr. Wharton mention the rent?"

"He said it would be a hundred and fifty dollars," replied Jean. "I rather think he was asking more from the Blores."

Although the former occupants had left the house in an untidy condition, floors and walls were in fairly good shape. Mrs. MacVey, wandering about by herself, found the arrangement of the rooms pleasing.

"I certainly shall take the house," she decided at last, and came to find the girls. "I think I've seen everything now," she said to Jean, realizing that they had spent a long while in the house.

"I wonder what became of Louise?" asked Jean.

"She was in the library a moment ago," replied the woman.

Going to the next room, the younger Dana called her sister, but Louise was not there. She

called again, louder this time. Her own voice
echoed back from the empty corridors, but there
was no other reply.

"Louise must be here somewhere," insisted
Mrs. MacVey. "Maybe she went outdoors."

The two looked in the garden, then went
through the house from cellar to attic. There
was no sign of the missing girl. It was rapidly
growing dark, and since the electric lights could
not be turned on, the searchers soon would be
compelled to give up.

"I don't know what to do now," Jean confessed in alarm. "I should return to Starhurst
but I can't until Louise is found. Oh, dear, I
am afraid something dreadful has happened
to her!"

CHAPTER VIII

Searching for Louise

Mrs. MacVey tried to comfort Jean by assuring the girl that her sister surely would be found soon. It was quite possible, she thought, that Louise had gone back to Starhurst School.

"I can't believe she would leave here without telling me, though," answered Jean soberly. "She always tries to avoid causing anyone worry."

"We've heard no one enter or leave the house," said her companion. "I can't understand it."

"I can't understand it myself, Mrs. MacVey. My sister just seemed to vanish into thin air."

By this time it was so dark inside the house that Jean and the woman had difficulty in groping their way about. Without candles or flashlights they could not hope to conduct an efficient search. However, they were both fairly well satisfied that Louise was nowhere upon the premises.

"I believe she must have returned to the school," Mrs. MacVey repeated again. "Suppose we go back there and see. If she hasn't appeared then, we'll notify the police."

64

"Very well," Jean agreed reluctantly.

The girl locked the house and returned to Mrs. MacVey's automobile which had been parked on the gravel driveway. Opening the rear door of the car, Jean gave a gasp of astonishment. Louise was curled up on the back seat sound asleep.

"Here she is, Mrs. MacVey!" her sister cried in delight. "Thank goodness, we've found her at last!"

"Well, that is a relief," murmured the woman, gazing down at the sleeping form.

"Louise!" Jean gave her sister a little shake. "Wake up!"

The girl did not stir.

"She sleeps soundly," observed Mrs. MacVey. "I suppose she became worn out from waiting so long. I should have had more consideration."

Jean shook Louise again but there was no response.

"What can be the matter with her, Mrs. MacVey?" she asked.

For just an instant Jean was terrified. It was not natural for Louise to sleep so soundly. Bending over the girl, she could hear her soft, regular breathing. She thought too that she detected a faint odor about her sister's clothing.

"Let me see if I can awaken her," offered Mrs. MacVey, taking Jean's place.

She shook the girl hard, slapping her wrists and cheeks several times. Louise stirred and groaned but did not open her eyes.

"Well, that is queer, I must say," the woman remarked.

As Jean nodded, she started to remark that perhaps Louise was under the influence of either a drug or a sleeping potion, but checked herself. It was just as well to keep such thoughts to one's self.

"I believe it will be better not to try to awaken her until we reach the school," Mrs. MacVey decided after a moment. "Perhaps she is merely exhausted from her long wait."

The woman drove immediately to Starhurst School. There Louise was aroused sufficiently to be led to her room. Mrs. MacVey, assuming that everything would be all right, took leave of Jean.

Her sister promptly collapsed on the bed, going off into further sound sleep. Throughout the night Jean sat beside her, watching nervously.

"I suppose I should call Mrs. Crandall," she told herself, "yet I dislike to. She'll never let us leave Starhurst again! I believe Louise has been drugged and that the effect will pass off soon. If she isn't better in the morning I'll tell the nurse."

To Jean's relief dawn did bring an improvement in her sister's condition. As the first rays of morning light filtered in, the sleeping girl stirred and yawned. Instantly her sister was at her side again.

"Louise!"

"Up so early, Jean?" she mumbled drowsily, as her heavy eyelids fluttered open. "What time is it?"

"Five o'clock. I've been awake all night. How do you feel?"

Louise raised herself on one elbow and gazed about the room in bewildered fashion.

"My, that was a horrible nightmare I had," she said without answering her sister's question. "I thought I was back in Mr. Wharton's house. Strange animals were chasing me, and then I seemed to be on a merry-go-round. I was talking with one of the wooden zebras if you'll believe me!"

"Never mind the nightmare, Louise. How do you feel?"

"Why, all right, I guess. My head aches a little. What is the matter, Jean? You're looking at me so strangely."

"Don't you remember a thing?"

"About what?" inquired Louise blankly.

"Why, about visiting Mr. Wharton's house, of course."

"Oh, yes, we did go there, didn't we? But I can't seem to remember whether or not Mrs. MacVey decided to take the place."

"She plans to move in day after tomorrow,

but that is beside the point. I've been worried half to death about you.''

''About me?''

''You don't seem to realize that you've been sleeping for nearly twelve hours,'' said Jean. ''Mrs. MacVey and I found you in the car. How did you get there?''

''I'm sure I don't know.''

''What is the last thing you remember?''

''Well, let me think. I became tired of waiting, so I walked into another part of the house.''

''Which room, Louise?''

''I can't tell you that either. My mind is a blank.''

''Now I'm sure you were drugged!''

''Drugged?'' asked Louise unbelievingly. ''I don't see how that would have been possible. I met no one in the house. I admit, though, I do feel queer.''

''Perhaps you picked up something and ate it —pills, for instance.''

''Now would I be likely to do anything as silly as that?''

''Then what did happen?'' insisted Jean.

''I tell you I don't know,'' Louise answered wearily, climbing out of bed. ''I refuse to worry about it anyway.''

As she went down the hall to take an ice cold shower, Jean, somewhat exasperated by her sister's matter-of-fact attitude, returned to bed, hoping to catch a few minutes of sleep. When the rising bell rang at six-thirty, Louise appeared far more rested than she did.

Very little was said about the incident later for neither of the girls could offer a plausible theory as to what had occurred in the Wharton house. Their time and thoughts became occupied with new interests. Jean was absorbed with her invention, and besides had promised to take part in a swimming meet between the Penfield Y.W.C.A. and Starhurst.

Both Dana girls were excellent swimmers while Evelyn Starr had become a proficient fancy diver. In fact, the only weak member on their team of six was Lettie Briggs.

The Starhurst girls arrived at the Y.W.C.A. building rather fearful of defeat, but after a few events had been run off, it became evident they would win by a large number of points. Jean and Louise earned themselves many first places. Lettie managed to trail behind in every race.

"Well, Lettie, this is your last chance to win a place," Jean said good-naturedly as the two lined up side by side at the pool's edge against their two opponents. "I really hope you win this time."

"Don't worry, I shall," retorted the girl irritably. "Just see that you keep out of my way."

The starting signal was given and the four swimmers dived into the water at the same instant. Lettie and Jean quickly forged ahead of the others, racing for a time side by side. Then slowly the Dana girl began to move ahead. Lettie redoubled her efforts and crowded so close to Jean that their bodies touched as they swam.

When they finished the race, the unpleasant girl was a yard behind Jean.

"Well, I guess I won," she announced triumphantly. "You'll be disqualified, Jean, for pushing against me!"

"It was you who should be ruled out of the race," replied Jean coolly.

"Miss Briggs—disqualified for being out of her lane!" called an official, giving his ruling in a loud voice. "Winner, Miss Jean Dana. Second, Miss Thomas. Third, Miss Smith."

Lettie ran to the official to complain but he would not listen to her. Then the girl lost her temper completely and demanded that the decision be reversed. Her protests were ignored. In the dressing room everyone grew weary listening to her excited claim that she had been "cheated out of the race."

"Let's go outside and wait for the other girls," Jean whispered to her sister. "I am tired of hearing Lettie say the same thing over and over."

As the Dana girls emerged from the gymnasium, they noticed a speeding car coming down the street. Tires screamed protestingly as it skidded around a corner.

"Jean!" cried Louise. "That looks like the car which carried Charlie Young away!"

"The license number *is* the same! Louise, we must catch that driver!"

Frantically the girls glanced about for a taxi cab. None was in sight, but at that moment one of the instructors who had attended the swimming meet came from the gymnasium. His car was parked at the curb.

"Oh, Mr. Halley," Jean said, hurrying toward him, "will you take us in your car and catch that auto ahead? It's very important." She indicated the vanishing speeder.

"I have an errand," he replied, "but you may take my car. Be sure to come right back."

He dropped the keys into the girl's hand. Jean and Louise sprang into the car and had the engine started in a twinkling. Before the other automobile had gone three blocks, they had caught up with it.

"It's the same man who kidnaped Charlie Young," Louise declared with conviction. "He seems to be heading toward the river."

"We must trail him!" declared Jean.

The girls followed the car for perhaps a mile, where it drew up along the banks of the Avon River. The man alighted, and locating a boat which had been hidden at the water's edge, rowed rapidly downstream.

In his haste the stranger failed to observe a group of boys who were fishing from a skiff close to shore. Before the Dana girls could call out a warning the two boats collided.

The skiff, with its cargo of screaming boys, righted itself, but the man was hurled into the stream. Beating water with his hands, he called feebly for help. The boys seemed too frightened to be of any aid.

"That man can't swim a stroke!" cried Jean, springing from the car. "Louise, we must save him!"

CHAPTER IX

A RESCUE

STOPPING only long enough to kick off their shoes, the Dana girls plunged into the waters of the swiftly racing stream. A few powerful strokes brought them close to the struggling man.

By this time the small boys in the nearby skiff were attempting to be of assistance. One lad was standing in the boat, trying to extend an oar to the drowning man.

"Be careful!" called Louise, but she spoke too late.

Suddenly the over-weighted craft capsized, pitching its occupants into the water. In a moment it became evident that some of the little fellows could not swim. Louise and Jean were confronted with a desperate situation, and had they not remained calm, disaster certainly would have followed.

Fortunately two of the boys could swim a few strokes and succeeded in reaching the over-turned skiff. Louise helped the others to safety, instructing them how to cling to the floating craft.

Jean, meanwhile, was having difficulties with the struggling man. As she reached out to take his arm, he suddenly tried to seize her in a strangle hold. For several moments she was hard pressed to keep from being pulled under the surface. At last, however, she secured a safe grip and started to tow him to shore.

Louise managed to bring the skiff and the four boys who clung to its sides into shallow water. From there they were able to wade to the beach.

"Where do you live?" she asked them, knowing they must get into dry clothes.

"I live over there," answered one of the lads. He pointed to a farmhouse visible on a hilltop.

"Then climb in the car. I'll drive you home."

Louise turned to see what her sister was doing. The man she had brought to shore was sitting on the ground, staring blankly.

"He swallowed a little water," said Jean, "but I think he will be all right."

The man pressed his hands against his stomach and a look of pain came over his face.

"Are you ill?" inquired Louise sympathetically.

"I feel awful."

"That's because you swallowed so much river water," Jean told him. "The discomfort shouldn't last long."

"You saved me?" the man inquired, staring stupidly at the girl.

"Yes, I brought you ashore. It would have

been much easier if you hadn't struggled so hard."

"I couldn't help it," the man muttered. "Thanks for pulling me out."

"I was glad to do it," Jean replied.

"We'll take you over to that house yonder," Louise offered after a moment. "You mustn't sit here on the beach in wet clothing."

Her words seemed to arouse the man. He struggled to his feet.

"I am feeling better now—much better. Don't bother about me."

Before the Dana girls could protest, he staggered off to his own car and drove away.

"We should have kept him," Jean said self-accusingly.

"He's in no state to be questioned now, Jean. Anyway, we must take these boys to their homes."

Considerable time elapsed before the girls delivered their last passenger, but finally they returned to the Penfield Y.W.C.A. gymnasium. Upon giving an account of their adventure they were praised for the rescue, but Mrs. Crandall added a word of warning to the effect that it was unwise to become involved with a stranger.

"It is just as well the man did drive away," she declared. "After all, you may have been mistaken in thinking him to be the person who kidnapped Charlie Young."

Louise and Jean were confident their identification had been correct, but they said no more about the matter. The following day, which was Saturday, they returned to the Wharton house to offer their services to Mrs. MacVey, who was moving in. When the girls arrived, a large van already stood at the door.

"The family's not here yet," the driver complained. "We've been waiting twenty minutes and we want to get started unloading."

"I have a key," said Jean, taking it from her pocket. "Mr. Wharton gave it to me."

She unlocked the door and helped her sister place heavy paper on the floors so they would not be scratched.

"Now, Louise, I hope you don't wander away again and get into another trance," she remarked jokingly. "Shall I keep my eye upon you all the time?"

"It won't be necessary, thanks."

While the girls were telling the movers where to set some of the furniture, a taxi cab rolled up the driveway.

"That must be Mrs. MacVey now," Jean said in relief.

The girls hastened outside, but to their surprise it was old Mr. Wharton who stepped from the cab. As he was leaning heavily on a cane, they ran to help him.

"Oh, Mr. Wharton, it's good to see you again," Louise said cordially. "Are you really strong enough to have made this trip?"

"Tut and nonsense! I'll soon be as well as ever. I came to make certain everything is all right here. Has the water been turned on?"

"Yes, the man was here ten minutes ago," replied Louise.

"Then we'll test the taps to be sure there are no leaks."

"Everything seems to be all right," Jean said, helping the invalid up the porch steps.

"I'll just look around a bit anyhow," the old man declared. "No telling how much damage those Blores may have done."

While Jean and Louise returned to their task of informing the movers where to set furniture, Mr. Wharton wandered about the house. The girls heard him down in the basement turning on faucets. A little later his cane was tapping across the bare floors of the second story.

They lost track of him entirely after the arrival of the MacVey family. Their car had been delayed because of a flat tire, and Mrs. MacVey was in a highly flustered state.

"Oh, dear, everything has gone wrong this morning!" she exclaimed. "The children are so excited, and my poor head is in a whirl!"

"Jean and I will help all we can."

"You've done so much already. But I'll appreciate it if you will just keep an eye on the children."

Keeping an eye upon Bennie, Barbara, Gloria, Donald, and the twins, Dave and Dot, proved to be a task indeed. The children were not intentionally mischievous but they had been reared by a mother who believed in allowing them to express themselves.

They raced madly through the house, exploring each room and getting in the way of the movers. In search of their toys they would take articles from the barrels, tossing them helter-skelter on the floor. Donald was discovered wading in the little brook which crossed the Wharton property.

"We need at least two sets of eyes and about six extra hands," sighed Jean to her sister. "Mrs. MacVey must have a wonderful constitution or she would have been in a sanatorium long ago."

Finally, at their wits ends, the Dana girls organized a strenuous game of tag which kept all the children occupied and within view. At the end they were more worn out than the boys and girls!

By noon all the furniture was in place. After the movers had driven away, the children became quiet, so Jean and Louise found time to help Mrs. MacVey prepare a hot luncheon.

"I wonder what became of Mr. Wharton?" Jean inquired as she set the table.

"I was talking with him a few minutes ago," mentioned Mrs. MacVey. "He seems like a very nice old gentleman, but he doesn't look strong."

"He suffered a heart attack recently," explained Louise. "I really think he shouldn't have made this trip."

"Do you suppose he would like to take lunch with us?"

"I am sure he would," declared Jean instantly.

"Then will you and Louise invite him, while I see that the children do a little scrubbing up."

The Dana girls went through the house but could not find Mr. Wharton anywhere. Nor were they able to locate him on the grounds.

"Perhaps he returned to the inn," Jean said, looking troubled.

"He couldn't have gone without calling a taxi. We would have seen one if it had driven up."

"Yes, you are right, Louise. Mr. Wharton must be here somewhere."

The sisters were worried as they returned in a little while to tell Mrs. MacVey that they were unable to find the old gentleman. Since they could not believe he had left the premises, they slipped quietly from the house while the MacVeys were at luncheon.

"Louise, I am afraid something has happened to him," Jean said anxiously. "He may have had another heart attack."

Although the girls called Mr. Wharton's name again and again, there was no response. After making a complete tour of the grounds they were forced to admit that it was useless to search further.

"I guess he did go back to the inn," Louise acknowledged unwillingly.

Jean, who had been walking slightly ahead of her sister, suddenly stopped. With a little cry of alarm she ran toward a clump of syringa bushes near the house.

"What do you see?" cried Louise quickly.

Without answering her sister indicated an object which lay on the ground.

"Mr. Wharton's cane!"

"Yes, and we've found him too, Louise. Oh, I was afraid of this!"

Jean had parted the bushes. Lying on the ground in a crumpled heap was the old gentleman. His face was deathly white and he scarcely seemed to breathe.

CHAPTER X

A Strange Trance

"Is—is he dead?" whispered Louise as her sister bent over the old man.

"No, I can see he is breathing," Jean replied in relief.

"He must have had another heart attack. We must get a doctor at once."

Jean knelt down to feel Mr. Wharton's pulse. It was fairly strong.

"Louise, I don't believe it's a heart attack at all."

"Then what can be the matter with him?"

"I found you in the same condition, Louise," Jean told her gravely. "Mr. Wharton is in a sort of trance just as you were!"

"He does appear to be sleeping peacefully. But his face is so white, it frightens me."

"The old gentleman was very pale when he came here this morning. If we can get him back to his hotel I believe he will be all right."

"I'll call Mr. MacVey," Louise said, starting away.

In a moment she came back with both the man and his wife, who urged that the old man be carried into their house.

81

"I think it might be better to take him back to his hotel," Jean suggested quietly. "We could get him there all right if we could borrow your car."

"Yes, that would be best," Mrs. MacVey decided after a moment. "We are so unsettled here, and I never can keep the children quiet. Poor Mr. Wharton! Another heart attack, of course."

The Danas did not correct the impression, for they thought it would be unwise to alarm the new tenants by revealing their fears. The couple would be almost certain to decide that the Wharton property had been "jinxed." Fortunately Mrs. MacVey did not seem to connect Mr. Wharton's strange seizure with the attack Louise had suffered.

Her husband helped the girls lift the old man into the car. He continued to sleep peacefully although his eyelids fluttered open once for an instant.

"I'll go with you," Mr. MacVey offered.

They drove to the Beckworth Inn and with the aid of the hotel people were able to get old Mr. Wharton to his room. Few questions were asked, for it was assumed that the man had suffered a relapse.

Satisfied that a nurse would look after the patient, the Dana girls returned to the mysterious house. Since Mr. MacVey accompanied them they could not discuss what was in their

minds, but both Louise and Jean were determined to make a thorough investigation of the
property at the first opportunity. They found
Mrs. MacVey in the library unpacking books.

"I like this old house better every minute,"
the woman declared cheerfully after inquiring
about Mr. Wharton's condition. "This is the
first time in years we have had ample shelf
space for our books."

"You have a great many," observed Louise,
counting the ten large boxes.

"You must have hundreds of them," said
Jean.

"Yes, the children all like to read. Then my
husband's hobby is gardening, and he always is
buying a new book about plants."

"Have you any devoted to rare herbs?"
Louise asked suddenly.

"It seems to me we have. You might look in
that box over by the window. It contains nearly
all of the gardening books."

Louise started to unpack the box, examining
each book carefully. Jean decided to help, for
it had dawned upon her why her sister had become interested in herbs.

"You believe that Mr. Wharton may have
been drugged by a strange weed or plant growing around here, don't you?" she whispered.

"Yes, I can't explain it any other way,"
Louise replied in an undertone.

After searching halfway through the box of

books she came upon one which interested her. Its title was, "Poisonous Plants and Herbs of North America."

"If you find anything which looks worth while, take it back to school with you," Mrs. MacVey suggested carelessly. "Or do your teachers keep you busy reading?"

"They manage to do that," returned Louise, smiling. "But I should like to borrow this book."

"Take it along, and don't be in a hurry about returning it."

The girls thanked the woman and carried the book to the front porch. As the volume was illustrated with beautiful colored pictures, the four older MacVey children soon gathered to look at them.

"Oh, I know that shrub," boasted Bennie, pointing to one of the photographs. "It's poison sumac and if you eat the berries you get real sick!"

"Have you seen any of it growing on the grounds?" asked Jean quickly.

"No, but I saw some poison ivy," the boy declared. "And there are other plants just like the pictures, only I don't know their names."

"Bennie, how would you like to play a little game?" asked Louise.

"Doing what?"

"We'll identify the leaves of different plants

and herbs. You children gather them and bring them here.''

''That would be fun,'' Bennie said, his eyes dancing.

As the other children wished to play also, they started off in various directions to find the herbs.

''Don't touch anything that looks like poison ivy,'' Jean called in warning. ''And be careful not to chew any plant leaves.''

Soon the youngsters came running back with their collection. Many of the plants were common weeds easily recognized, but Bennie brought several herbs which could not be identified. As it was growing late, the Dana girls decided regretfully that they could spend no more time on the game. They must return to school.

''I'll take the book and these herbs with me,'' Louise told the children. ''Next time I come I'll be able to tell you all the names.''

''We'll find some new ones for you, too,'' Bennie promised gaily.

At Starhurst once more, Louise spent many hours over the volume on herbs. She mounted her specimens in a notebook and wrote out a brief history of each plant.

''Have you found one that will produce a deep sleep?'' inquired Jean.

''Not yet, but it will take me a long while to read the entire book.''

Jean was content to have her sister struggle

with the problem of identifying poisonous herbs, for her own hours were engrossed with the music machine. True to his promise, Captain Dana had mailed to his niece several heavyweight springs which were more suitable than the ones she had been using. Upon installing them, Jean noted an improvement in the mechanism, but still the gadget would not work properly.

"I am sure it is just some little thing that is wrong," she declared optimistically. "I'll keep working and one of these days success may be mine!"

One afternoon while the Dana girls were absorbed with their hobbies, Mrs. Crandall dropped into their suite. She displayed a deep interest in Jean's invention, saying that if ever it were perfected, it would prove of great value to the school. Likewise she nodded approvingly as she saw Louise's notebook.

"Very commendable," she remarked.

So impressed was the headmistress, that at assembly the following morning she suggested it might be worthwhile for every girl to have an instructive hobby.

"Perhaps we do have!" said Lettie in a half-whisper which carried farther than she had intended.

"Yes, I imagine many of you are absorbed in fascinating pursuits," went on Mrs. Crandall, glancing at Lettie. "I shall ask each girl to submit a theme tomorrow about her favorite hobby. Shall we say five hundred words?''

A gloomy silence greeted the announcement, for very few of the students enjoyed writing themes. Nearly everyone blamed Lettie for the disaster which had come upon them, while she in turn sought to place the responsibility upon the Dana girls.

''I'll not write a theme about hobbies,'' she declared angrily. ''I'll tell about my pets instead.''

''Meaning your white mice?'' suggested someone mischievously.

Lettie's face flushed, and to escape the general laughter, the girl hastily retreated to her room.

The next day the Danas were pleased to receive a letter from their Uncle Ned. They had written him of their failure to locate Charlie Young, and he replied that the steamship company was having no better luck in tracing Katherine Blore. He would have no opportunity to do any investigating himself, as a scheduled voyage required his immediate return to New York.

''I wish we could gather a few clues while Uncle Ned is away,'' Jean remarked as she folded the letter. ''It is too bad we weren't able to question that stranger who fell into the river.''

''Yes, it is, but I have another idea.''

''Let's hear it, Louise.''

"The other day when I was in Penfield I noticed a laundry operated by a fellow who calls himself Wu Sing. Perhaps he could tell us something about his countryman Charlie Young."

"It's worth trying at least," agreed Jean instantly.

Later that day the Dana girls presented themselves at the establishment of Wu Sing. Entering quietly, they noticed that the front room was deserted. From the rear of the shop they could hear someone talking.

"I wonder if that could be——"

Jean too thought that she recognized the lower pitched voice. Tiptoeing across the room, she gazed into the rear compartment of the shop. Wu Sing was holding an excited conversation with a tall dark man whom the girl knew instantly.

"What luck!" she whispered excitedly to Louise. "It is that same man we pulled from the river, the one who carried Charlie Young away!"

CHAPTER XI

The Student's Clue

Louise and Jean could not hear everything the two men were saying, but they caught enough to follow the trend of the conversation. It became clear to them that the young China-man, Wu Sing, had entered the United States illegally, and that the stranger, Ed Newsome, was forcing him to pay hush money to keep from having the facts revealed.

"You come tomollow again," the laundryman sighed wearily. "Maybe then Wu Sing have money for you."

"All right," Newsome replied irritably, "but mind, no more stalling. Either you'll pay—or else——"

Without completing the threat, he turned to walk toward the door. The girls barely had time to step out of sight. As he came into the room, the man scarcely noticed them, but Jean deliberately blocked the exit.

"Aren't you the person I saved from the river?" she inquired sweetly.

Newsome stopped to stare at the girl. A frown wrinkled his forehead but it was gone in an instant.

"Oh, yes, yes, that's right," he answered uneasily. "I didn't recognize you for a moment. The light is poor in here."

Wu Sing had followed the man from the rear room and was gazing at the Danas curiously. Feeling that an introduction was expected of him, Newsome said in an off-hand way:

"Wu Sing, these young ladies saved me from a watery grave the other day when my boat upset. Let me see, do I know your names?"

"Louise and Jean Dana. And yours?"

"Ed Newsome," the man replied reluctantly.

The girls spoke politely to Wu Sing who bestowed upon them his most gracious smile.

"Young ladies do velly good deed! Velly good deed!" Then the Oriental turned his head, muttering words not intended for Newsome's ears. However, the girls thought they heard him say, "Bad rubbish, he all time get saved!"

"I'll remember that," thought Louise.

The man was becoming increasingly uncomfortable and eager to be away. The Dana girls had no intention of allowing him to elude them. Jean still stood in the doorway.

"I wonder if by chance you are acquainted with Charlie Young?" she said to Wu Sing. "He formerly was employed at the David Blore home."

The laundryman shook his head.

"Wu Sing not know Charlie Young. Maybe

he velly young China boy. Wu Sing not know many honorable countrymen.''

"It is very important that the man be found," contributed Louise, her gaze upon the other man.

"Maybe Mr. Newsome know him," said Wu Sing slyly. "In my country is velly old-wise saying, 'To find lost boy, send man to whom he owes much silver.' ''

"So Charlie Young owes you money, Mr. Newsome?" inquired Louise innocently.

She thought she understood what Wu Sing had meant to imply. Undoubtedly Charlie Young also had entered the United States illegally and was paying hush money to keep the information from being given to the authorities.

"Wu Sing will have his joke," laughed Ed Newsome in a hollow tone.

"But you do know Charlie Young?" asked Jean.

"Oh, I've seen him once or twice," the man answered evasively.

"Where is he now?" questioned Louise.

"Out West."

"In the West!" exclaimed Louise incredulously. "How did he get there?"

"The Blores took him with them to their ranch," replied the man, edging nearer the door.

"Where is their ranch?" Jean scarcely knew whether or not to believe the man.

"Somewhere near Slipper Creek."

With a muttered excuse that he had to catch a train, Newsome pushed Jean rudely aside and hurried out the door. Before the Dana girls could question Wu Sing other customers came into the laundry. The Chinese was kept so busy that Louise and Jean saw they would have no opportunity to talk privately with him for a long while. Accordingly they returned to Starhurst School, where they went directly to the library.

"Now to find Slipper Creek on the map!" Jean declared, selecting a large atlas from the shelf.

"I'll venture it is an imaginary name."

"Mr. Ed Newsome may have made it up on the spur of the moment. It would be in keeping with his character."

"What state shall we try?" inquired Louise as they pored over the atlas.

"We might try Wyoming."

A search of the state did not reveal the name of Slipper Creek. The girls tried Montana, Arizona, Texas.

"I don't believe there is such a place!" Jean exclaimed. "We might have known he would make it up!"

"I guess he did," agreed her sister.

Just then a dark-haired girl who wore tailored clothes came into the library. The Danas were acquainted with her only slightly, for Frances

Roy was a new student who had arrived at the school only the previous month.

"Such industry!" the newcomer remarked with a friendly smile. "Do you girls always spend your spare time studying?"

"Oh, we're not working now," Louise explained quickly. "We're trying to find a place on the map."

"It's supposed to be a ranch in the West," added Jean, "but I doubt if there is any such place as Slipper Creek."

"Slipper Creek!" echoed Frances in a startled voice.

"Did you ever hear of it?" asked Louise eagerly.

"Well, rather. I come from the West, you know."

"You do?" Jean inquired in delight. "Which state?"

"New Mexico. And Slipper Creek isn't the name of a town or a ranch. It is a small river which flows near my father's property. I doubt you'll find it on a map."

"Frances, did you ever hear of anyone by the name of David Blore?" Louise questioned abruptly.

"Why, yes. His ranch is about eight miles from our place. Their cattle carry the Bar II brand. The ranch has been allowed to run down terribly, though, because Mr. Blore is seldom at home."

"Who stays at the ranch when he's away?" inquired Jean.

"Old Mrs. Blore, his mother, and a few cowboys. I used to ride over and visit her occasionally. She is a very lonely woman."

"Has she a Chinese cook or a butler named Charlie Young?" questioned Louise thoughtfully.

"Not to my knowledge. The last time I was there she had a colored man cooking for the boys at the bunk-house."

"Of course it's possible that Charlie Young could have been taken to the ranch for the first time this past week," Jean commented slowly. "In that case you wouldn't have known about him or seen him there."

"True," admitted Frances. "See here, do you girls really want to find out about this Chinaman?"

"Yes, we do," Louise replied instantly.

"Then I'll tell you what I'll do. If you like, I'll telegraph my parents and ask them for information."

"Oh, we'd appreciate that more than we can tell you!" cried Jean. "Will you inquire if either Charlie Young or the Blores have shown up at the ranch?"

"You girls might help me with the telegram," suggested Frances. "I never was very good at wording messages."

The Danas were only too glad to compose the wire. The next morning they carried it to a telegraph office at Penfield, then went to the Beckworth Inn to inquire regarding Mr. Wharton's health. They were relieved to learn that the old man had aroused from his stupor and seemed to be in normal condition.

"The same thing must have happened to him that did to you, Louise," Jean said thoughtfully. "But what could it have been?"

"I confidently believe we both were poisoned by some sort of shrub or herb," responded her sister.

"Whatever it is, it's a dangerous drug to be left around," said Jean.

"You're right," agreed Louise, "and the sooner we can solve the mystery, the better."

"Mysteries certainly are crowding in on us," laughed the younger Dana.

The girls crossed the street intending to catch a return bus to Starhurst School. As they waited at the stop sign they were surprised to see Mrs. MacVey hastening toward them.

"I wonder what can be wrong now?" Jean asked, noticing the woman's agitated face. "She appears dreadfully upset."

As the woman came up to them, she cried excitedly, "Oh hello, girls. I'm looking for a drug store! Can you tell me how to find one?"

"Clayton's is two blocks to your left," replied Louise. "What is wrong, Mrs. MacVey?"

The woman turned a tear-stained face toward the Dana girls.

"It's little Donald," she said brokenly. "I couldn't wake him up this morning. He has a strange sleeping sickness, and I am afraid he may die!"

CHAPTER XII

MRS. MACVEY'S words startled the Danas. Instantly they guessed that little Donald had fallen into a sleep similar to the trance-like condition suffered by Mr. Wharton and Louise. Realizing that it would be cruel to withhold their knowledge, the girls said they believed the child's illness had been caused by an herb. They felt sure it would pass away soon without disastrous results.

"Don't you recall," Jean said comfortingly, "that Louise had the same thing? And also Mr. Wharton? They both recovered quickly."

"I thought he had a heart attack," protested Mrs. MacVey.

"We doubt it very much," replied Louise. "This morning when we inquired at the inn the old gentleman seemed to be in normal condition. In fact, the long sleep strengthened him."

"Then you think Donald really isn't very ill?" the anxious mother asked.

"I am certain of it," replied Jean confidently. "If I were in your place I should allow him to sleep undisturbed."

"Well, I do feel relieved," Mrs. MacVey sighed. "But what herb could have caused such a strange condition?"

"We don't know," confessed Louise frankly.

"We're making a study of poisonous herbs and plants," Jean added. "That is why we borrowed your book."

"Have you found anything yet which might explain the strange illness?"

"Not yet," Jean confessed ruefully, "but we'll keep working."

"I hesitate to remain in the house after this happening. One of the other children might get the same thing."

"We may stumble upon the explanation any day," Louise told her reassuringly. "It seems a pity to give up the house."

"Yes, it does. We like it so well. I suppose I can keep particularly close watch of the children for a while and then nothing can happen. Well, here comes your bus, girls. Good-bye, and many thanks."

"We really must get busy on that herb book now," Louise declared grimly as the girls rode back to school. "This affair threatens to become serious."

Between classes they applied themselves diligently to their task. Jean even abandoned work on her music machine, devoting every spare minute to the classification of poisonous herbs and plants. Despite their combined labors, the girls could find nothing which confirmed their theory.

"It's the strangest thing I ever knew," declared Louise.

Eagerly the Danas awaited a reply to the telegram which Frances Roy had sent to her parents. As considerable time had elapsed they began to fear that the people in New Mexico had been unable to answer their questions.

"I'll surely hear from them shortly," Frances told the girls. "My birthday is coming soon, on the next holiday, in fact, so I know they'll write to me by that time."

Jean and Louise discussed their own plans for the holiday. Since it would fall upon a Thursday they thought of asking Mrs. Crandall for permission to spend the week-end at their home in Oak Falls. While they were debating the matter, Frances Roy came bursting into their rooms, waving an air mail letter.

"I've heard from them at last!"

"Your parents?" cried Jean eagerly.

"Yes, they wrote instead of wiring because they had so much to say! How would you like to go out West with me?"

"Go West?" cried Louise. "But that would be impossible, Frances!"

"No, it wouldn't! My parents want me to come home for my birthday and they write I may invite you girls to go, too!"

Jean's eyes danced at the mere prospect of going to New Mexico, but in a moment she shook her head.

"Have you forgotten school, Frances? We would be gone weeks. And then there's the matter of car fare."

"Oh my, you're not modern at all!" laughed Frances. "Don't you ever think of traveling by airplane?"

"Yes," replied Louise with a smile, "and it's wonderful, but we're not wealthy."

"Oh, the fare is all arranged. Dad enclosed a check. He says we are to take the first plane West! Will you come as my guests?"

"We'd love to," Jean said breathlessly, "but——"

"No buts," interposed Frances briskly. "I've talked already with Mrs. Crandall, who is willing. All that is necessary now is the permission from your aunt."

"I think we can manage that," declared Louise confidently. "Oh, Frances, you're an angel to take us!"

"I'll enjoy the trip myself. And it will be a splendid opportunity for you to learn about your friends the Blores."

"They aren't friends," Jean corrected hastily. "Did your father say anything about them in his letter?"

"Yes, he writes they are at their ranch."

"Then we'll have a good chance to clear up

the mystery of Katherine Blore's disappearance from my uncle's ship," Louise cried gaily. "Oh, I'm sure Aunt Harriet will let us go now."

Upon learning of the invitation Miss Dana did decide that her nieces might make the trip to New Mexico. Not only would they have an enjoyable time, she thought, but they would have an opportunity to render a service to Captain Dana and the company for which he worked.

Only one detail stood between the girls and their prospective vacation. Mrs. Crandall had announced that examinations would be held during the early part of the following week, and it was her custom to deny privileges to any girl who fell below the general average. Louise and Jean were not worried on their own account, but they knew that Frances was having a difficult time with several subjects.

"I am afraid I shall fail in history," she confessed to the Danas. "I'll never get over the blow if we miss our trip on account of my grades."

"Would it help you if we review the work with you?" Jean asked suddenly, fearful that the vacation might have to be given up.

"Oh, yes! I never can tell the important things to remember by myself," replied the Western girl. "But I don't like to ask you to do it——"

"We'll be glad to help," Louise said quickly. "Suppose we start right away."

"Here?" asked Frances doubtfully. "I hate to have the girls know I am so stupid."

"We might go into the woods at the rear of the dormitory," suggested Jean. "No one will bother us there."

The chums took the needed books, then without telling anyone their destination, started for the woods. From the window of her room Lettie Briggs observed them leave.

"Now what are they going to do?" she asked herself curiously. "I'll just follow them and find out!"

Unaware that they had an eavesdropper, the Dana girls and Frances selected a pleasant site near the river. There they took turns reading aloud and commenting upon the text.

Lettie had hidden herself in a nearby clump of bushes. Fearing that she would miss information of vital importance, the girl listened to every word, even taking a few notes. Not until Louise closed the history book and arose to leave, did the listening Briggs girl realize that she had tricked herself.

"They aren't going to talk over secrets at all!" she thought in disgust. "To think I wasted my time that way!"

She started to steal away, angry with herself. Just then a garter snake crawled across the path in front of her. Terrified, Lettie gave a shrill scream which revealed her presence to the other girls.

"Why Lettie," said Jean in mock surprise, "imagine finding you here!"

"I am out for a walk," the girl stammered. "A—a great big snake over a yard long crawled across my foot!"

"Do you mean this little baby snake?" laughed Frances Roy, pointing to the reptile which had taken refuge under a plant.

"I—I thought it was a lot bigger than that."

"I am afraid you need a new pair of eyes," observed Louise dryly. "But nothing seems to be wrong with your ears!"

Due to the coaching of the Dana girls, Frances Roy passed her tests with fairly good grades. Indirectly Lettie benefited too, for in the review overheard by her, Louise and Jean had taken up nearly all the questions which were asked later in the history test.

"Nothing stands in our way now," Jean declared gaily when the marks were made known. "We'll soon be off for the West!"

"Let's start packing at once," proposed Louise eagerly. "I can hardly wait."

As they selected various kinds of clothing to take on the trip, Jean glanced regretfully at her invention.

"I wonder—" she started to say.

"You aren't planning to cart *that* along?" Louise asked quickly. "The airline allows a passenger only a certain amount of weight, you know."

"Oh, all right," laughed Jean good-naturedly. "But I'll miss my brain-child."

Just as the girls finished packing, one of their friends, Margaret Glenn, rapped on the door.

"You're wanted on the telephone," she told them. "The maid didn't say who it is."

"Do you suppose it can be Aunt Harriet, Jean?" Louise asked, as the two hurried down the hall. "I hope she hasn't changed her mind about the trip!"

"You answer it," urged her sister.

Louise took down the receiver. In a moment a queer expression went across her face.

"Yes, we'll try to do that," she promised after a moment. "Hello—hello—oh, he cut off."

"He? Who?"

Louise's eyes were bright with excitement as she faced her sister.

"That was Wu Sing!"

"Why was he calling us?"

"I don't know," answered Louise soberly, "but he must have important information, because he asked us to call at his place immediately!"

CHAPTER XIII

WESTWARD BOUND

"YOU promised Wu Sing we would call at his laundry?" Jean asked her sister, a tiny frown puckering her eyebrows.

"Why yes, of course. He may have important news for us about Charlie Young."

"I realize that, Louise. But have you forgotten the party?"

A group of friends headed by Evelyn Starr had planned a farewell gathering for Frances Roy, Louise and Jean. It was to be held that afternoon. Immediately after the party the three girls expected to take a taxi to the flying field, from which their plane would leave at four o'clock.

"We'll never have time to get everything in," Jean protested again.

"Then we must cut the party short. We can explain to Evelyn. I really think it's important that we see Wu Sing."

The gathering proved to be a very enjoyable one. The Danas were sorry when the time came for them to leave. Making their excuses to Evelyn and the others, they drew Frances Roy aside.

"We have an important errand in Penfield," Jean explained to her friend. "Will it be all right if we meet you at the airport?"

"Of course," the girl replied. "Just so you don't miss the plane. We haven't much time to spare even now."

"Louise and I will keep one eye on our watches. We'll be there without fail," Jean promised.

Saying farewell to their friends, the Dana girls took a taxi cab directly to the establishment of Wu Sing.

"I hope he won't take much time telling us what he has learned," Jean said anxiously. "We really are taking a chance in coming here."

"We'll have a half hour to reach the airport. That should be long enough."

Telling the taxi driver to wait, the girls entered the laundry. The front room was deserted of customers. They could hear Wu Sing moving about in the rear room, and in a moment he appeared.

"Wu Sing velly glad young ladies clome," he said with a broad smile. "Missees wish hear more about Charlie Young?"

"Yes, indeed we do," Louise replied eagerly. "What have you learned?"

"Small boys come see Wu Sing," the man began. "Tell how they find Charlie Young in shack-house on island. He tied up with ropes like wild animal. Young Amelicans crash-crash door and set Charlie free.''

"Where is this island?" Louise inquired quickly. "Near here?"

"Wu Sing not sure. Think maybe boys mean Avon River.''

The girls did not tell the laundryman what was in their minds. However, it instantly occurred to them that Ed Newsome might have been intending to visit the island at the time of his boat mishap. Having carried the butler away, he had confined him somewhere; that was logical.

"Where is Charlie now?" Jean inquired thoughtfully.

"Wu Sing have no idea."

"If you can trace him, we hope you will help him in every possible way," Louise urged. "My sister and I will be out of town for a few days or we would carry on the search ourselves."

"Charlie Young velly hard boy to clatch," said the Chinaman, shaking his head. "But Wu Sing try."

Jean, glancing at her watch, saw that time was slipping away fast.

"We have only twenty minutes to catch our plane, Louise," she warned her sister nervously.

Immediately the girls thanked Wu Sing for the information he had given them and ran to the waiting taxi cab.

"To the airport," Jean ordered the driver, "and hurry! We must catch the four o'clock."

As the car sped through the streets, the girls discussed the new situation which had developed.

"Wu Sing's news throws a different light upon everything," Louise said thoughtfully. "Charlie Young can't very well be on a western ranch and here at the same time."

"I imagine Mr. Newsome for some reason of his own told us Charlie was with the Blores," returned Jean. "He probably said it just to deceive us."

"At any rate we can't change our minds about the trip at this late hour. Even if we accomplish little, we'll have a glorious time in the West."

The taxi cab drew into the airport with ten minutes to spare. Frances Roy was pacing up and down nervously in front of the passenger station.

"Oh, I am glad you've come at last!" she exclaimed, running to meet the girls. "I was so afraid you'd miss the plane."

"We told you we would get here," laughed Jean. "Now what are we supposed to do with our luggage?"

"The man will carry it in. Everything has to be weighed. I understand the plane will be loaded heavily because every seat has been sold, and there is an extra amount of mail.''

"You lead the way, Frances, and we'll follow,'' declared Jean gaily.

The Dana girls registered at the office, giving their names, addresses and weights to the clerk. Going outdoors again they watched a steward place their luggage aboard a beautiful four-motored plane which was warming up on the runway.

"May we get in any time?'' asked Jean eagerly.

"Yes. A few people are aboard now,'' answered Frances. "The first ones had their choice of seats.''

As the girls started toward the steps, a short, stout man, coat flying in the breeze, came running past them toward the airplane.

"I guess he is afraid he'll be left behind,'' said Frances with a chuckle.

"He acts as if he had lost something,'' declared Louise, quickening her own step as she heard a call to the passengers to come aboard.

When they reached the plane they heard the man talking excitedly with the stewardess.

"You are quite sure my brown alligator bag isn't here? I've searched every other place! It must be!''

"I have examined the luggage again, Mr. Craven,'' replied the attractive young woman "The bag is not aboard this plane.''

"Then someone has stolen it!''

"I hope it did not contain valuables."

"Yes, it did. I am a diamond merchant from New York. If that bag has disappeared, I'll sue the line! They'll have to pay for the loss."

"The jewels probably will be found," the stewardess said soothingly. "When did you last see it?"

"I set it down in the station. I don't just remember where——"

By this time Frances and the Dana girls were standing at the doorway of the plane. They could not get in for Mr. Craven was blocking the entrance.

"I beg your pardon," said Louise unexpectedly. "As we were walking across the runway I saw a steward carrying a large brown bag toward a plane at the east side of the field."

"Number 17, south bound," supplied the stewardess. "It takes off just ahead of us."

"Was the bag made of alligator?" inquired the merchant hopefully.

"I believe it was."

"Then maybe it is mine. Thanks for the tip," he called, hastening across the field toward the other plane.

The stewardess turned her attention to the girls, taking their coats and offering them magazines and chewing gum after they had found seats at the rear of the cabin.

"I wonder if Mr. Craven will miss his

plane?'' Louise remarked, peering out the window. ''I'll never forgive myself if I made a mistake about that bag.''

In a minute or two she was relieved to see the man hurrying back, accompanied by a steward who carried a brown suitcase.

''I found it all right,'' the jeweler gasped triumphantly as he sat down near the girls.

Recovering his breath, the man thanked Louise so profusely that she became embarrassed. She was glad when the cabin door slammed shut, and the plane prepared to take off.

As the engines started, another man was observed running across the field. He raised his hand in signal to the pilot who immediately cut the motors.

''I wonder why we stopped?'' murmured the stewardess, opening the cabin door. ''All my passengers are here, sir,'' she said to the newcomer.

''I'm Detective Cranshaw, Miss,'' said the man in a whisper. ''I am looking for a swindler. My orders are to search every plane.''

The stewardess stood aside, allowing the detective to enter the ship.

''Maybe he is after you, Louise,'' Jean whispered mischievously. ''Have you robbed any banks lately?''

The detective moved slowly up the aisle, carefully gazing at each passenger. Apparently satisfied that the person he wanted was not aboard, he apologized to the stewardess for the delay, and left the plane.

Again the stewardess closed the cabin door, but a few minutes later as the engines were warming up for the take-off, an old lady passenger in the fore part of the ship began to protest in a loud voice:

"I've changed my mind! I want to get off this plane!"

The stewardess was at the woman's side in an instant.

"Why, Mrs. Bennington?" she inquired. "Is anything wrong? You are not feeling ill?"

"I am feeling all right," the old lady answered tartly. "But I just know something will go wrong on this trip. That delay in the take-off is an ill omen."

"Oh, I can't agree with you," said the stewardess soothingly. "We often have delays. I have traveled over five hundred thousand miles by air without any trouble."

"Really?" asked the old lady, settling back into her chair. "This is my first trip. Well, I suppose I may as well go on."

This decision struck the Dana girls as somewhat amusing, for Mrs. Bennington could not have left the plane had she wished. Already it was rushing down the field, gathering speed for the take-off.

It seemed to Louise and Jean that the plane

was slow in leaving the ground. Once it rose for an instant and then settled. They were nearing the end of the field!

Recalling that Frances had told them the ship would be loaded to capacity, the girls turned to glance questioningly at the stewardess. The young woman had taken her usual place at the rear of the cabin. Her face was composed, but as she looked out the window, they saw that she sat rigidly, her fingers gripping the seat.

Instinctively they knew that while the young woman was trying not to alarm her passengers, she herself was afraid. There was every possibility that instead of rising, the plane might have a disastrous crash!

CHAPTER XIV

A CLOSE CALL

AFTER a few uncertain moments, the plane finally rose slowly from the runway just in time. Then, gathering power, it climbed steadily. The stewardess took a deep breath and smiled. Jean and Louise relaxed in their seats. The danger was over!

For a time the girls were absorbed in watching the scenery. The stewardess pointed out interesting places below, and when she was not occupied with Mrs. Bennington, who insisted the plane would crash at any minute, chatted with them. Learning that the girls were bound for the Slipper Creek locality, her interest became even more marked.

"I know that place very well," she declared enthusiastically. "I am engaged to a young man who has a ranch not far from there."

The stewardess went on to tell the girls that her fiance wished her to marry at once. She was trying to persuade him to postpone the wedding another three months.

"He'll be waiting for me at the end of the run," she admitted with a laugh. "I've promised to give him my answer then."

"Have you made up your mind?" inquired Frances Roy, curious.

"Not yet. But if I decide to have the wedding this week, I'll invite all of you!"

"I could provide the ring," chuckled Mr. Craven, who had overheard the conversation. "I have a very good-looking sample in my bag, one with an orange blossom design."

"We'll see," laughed Miss Brown. "I enjoy my work almost too well to leave it."

The journey by air was so pleasant that the Dana girls were sorry when at last the time came for them to bid their fellow passengers good-bye. The plane came down at the airport nearest Slipper Creek, then after a brief stop sped westward again.

"Oh, there is Dad now!" cried Frances, as a distinguished looking man in a sombrero hurried toward the girls. "I knew he would be here to meet us."

After Mr. Roy had gathered his daughter into his arms, he greeted Louise and Jean cordially.

"We'll get started for the ranch right away," he declared, carrying the girls' luggage to the waiting car.

After a lengthy ride through colorful canyons and green foothills, the party arrived at the Roy home. The Danas were welcomed by their chum's mother who loved young people. To the astonishment of Louise and Jean two tall, handsome college boys were introduced as Dick and Glenn, brothers of Frances.

"Why, you never told us you had any brothers," declared Jean.

"I thought I did," Frances answered carelessly. "Anyway, I hardly expected to see them here myself."

"Dad wrote us you were coming, Fran," said Dick with a grin. "We had to be here to celebrate your birthday."

"We'll have a grand time," Frances declared gaily. "This is wonderful!"

Dick and Glenn were pleasant young men, who at once made a point of planning a fine vacation for the Danas. They showed the girls the buildings and corral of the ranch, saddled horses for them to ride, and then asked:

"Any place in particular you would like to go?"

"Over to the Blore ranch," replied Louise. "We've heard a good bit about the people there."

"Oh yes, of course," said Dick.

"Let's ride over there tomorrow," suggested Frances. "We might take a picnic lunch with us."

"That would be fun," Jean agreed enthusiastically.

Early the next morning the girls packed knapsacks and took the trail for the Bar II Ranch. They rode alone, for Dick and Glenn were unable to accompany them, having duties at home. Enroute Frances pointed out many places of interest. The Danas were intrigued by the beauty of the spot.

"I am taking you the long way," she told the girls. "You're not in a hurry?"

"We're enjoying every minute of the ride," responded Louise enthusiastically.

At eleven o'clock the girls stopped under a shade tree to eat their lunch. They watered the horses at a brook, and then rode on slowly again. They had not gone far when Frances, who was ahead, suddenly drew rein.

"There is a break in the fence!" she exclaimed. "Our cattle are straying onto the Blore range!"

Frances pointed to a broken place in the barrier. Many of the cattle had escaped and others were trying to crowd through the gap.

Spurring her horse into action, Frances drove back the main herd, then set out to round up the strays. Quickly catching an idea of what their friend meant to do, Louise and Jean rode out to help her.

Several of the longhorns were stubborn and would bolt in the wrong direction. Jean had to gallop for some distance after one steer which was determined to elude her, but at last she succeeded in heading him off.

Finally all the animals were back on the Roy property once more. The girls drove them as

far from the gap in the fence as possible.
They then placed an old tree branch across the
break.

"That may hold them for a little while,"
Frances declared as the girls rested their
mounts. "When we reach the Blore ranch I'll
call home and tell Dad. He'll have the fence
mended right away."

"It looks to me as if these wires have been
cut," Jean observed, examining the broken
ends.

Quickly Frances went to her chum's side.

"They *have* been cut!" she exclaimed angrily. "Now who would do a trick like that?"

"Has your father any enemies?" inquired
Louise, scenting a mystery.

"Not to my knowledge. I can't understand
a thing like this."

As the three girls rode on toward the Bar II
Ranch, Frances became very thoughtful. Her
mind upon the problem of the broken fence,
she scarcely spoke.

At length, however, she drew rein at the top
of a hill, waiting for the Danas to come close.
With her riding crop she pointed toward the
east.

"See that grove of trees? Just beyond them
is the Blore ranch."

"The place looks deserted," observed Jean.

"The buildings are run down," replied Frances. "Mrs. Blore isn't able to look after things,

and the other members of the family take no interest."

"How many children has Mrs. Blore?" Louise inquired, her eyes upon the distant ranch buildings.

"None of her own. Dad tells me that Katherine and David were adopted."

"Really?" Jean questioned in surprise. "Well, that is certainly interesting to know."

"We may not be received very well if David and Katherine are at home," Louise remarked as the girls rode down the slope. "Perhaps it might be well to approach cautiously."

"We can go through the grove," proposed Frances. "In that way we'll not be seen until we are practically at the house."

Upon reaching the woods the girls dismounted and led their horses. As they drew near the homestead, Louise halted abruptly. Wondering what could be wrong, Jean and Frances likewise paused.

Then they saw why their companion had stopped. An old woman, with tears streaming down her withered cheeks, had come from the ranch house and was walking slowly toward the grove.

CHAPTER XV

A Dangerous Undertaking

"Is she Mrs. Blore?" Louise asked Frances in a low tone.

"Yes," replied the girl. Noticing a pail on the woman's arm, she added, "I imagine she is going to the spring for water. It is located here in the grove."

"Will we be seen?" questioned Jean. "We may frighten her."

"Not if we stay where we are."

"Someone is following Mrs. Blore!" Louise announced suddenly. "A man—why, he's David Blore!"

"Then we know he and his sister are at the ranch," Jean murmured. "Perhaps if we don't give ourselves away we'll learn something worth while."

As the girls peered through the gap in the trees, they saw the man overtake his mother. He spoke earnestly to her, but his words could not be heard. The old woman shook her head sadly, while tears kept streaming down her face.

"She acts positively heart-broken," Jean

whispered wonderingly. "What can be the matter?"

Mrs. Blore, followed by David, walked on to the spring which was very close to where the girls were standing. After filling her bucket the old woman sat down on a bench, half covering her face with her hand.

"There is nothing you can say to comfort me, David," she said sadly. "As a mother I have failed. I did try so hard to bring you and Katherine up the right way. My husband and I loved you as our own children, but you have disappointed us."

"How can you say a thing like that, Mother?" the man replied. "You don't understand."

"I understand far more than you realize, David. My husband and I slaved for you and Katherine, we educated you, and we tried to teach you to be honest and law abiding."

"You talk as if Katherine and I have committed some crime!"

"I don't know—I don't know," the old woman murmured brokenly. "You both say and do things which frighten me. Your constant demand for money——"

"Mother, you have lived on a ranch nearly all of your life," the man answered impatiently. "You don't seem to realize how much it takes to live decently."

"You both have grown extravagant."

"Katherine is beautiful and requires expen-

sive clothes," the man explained soothingly.
"As for myself, I have to keep up appearances
with my friends."

"Appearances! You would be far happier if
you were content to live simply."

"Your ways are not mine, Mother," returned David Blore wearily.

Before he could say more, the ranch house
dinner bell rang. With a tired sigh the old
woman arose. David picked up the bucket of
water and together they walked back.

"We seem to have arrived at an awkward
moment," Jean remarked after the couple had
disappeared into the house. "Just at meal
time."

"I suppose we should wait," acknowledged
Louise. "You're in no hurry, Frances?"

"No, except that I should like to telephone
my father about the fence."

"I had forgotten," Louise said, frowning in
perplexity.

"The Blores have a telephone in their bunk-
house," Frances recalled. "I'll slip in there
and use it. You girls wait here by the spring."

While the Danas tied their horses to nearby
trees, she slipped through the grove to the
bunk-house. Finding it deserted, she made her
telephone call. Then without being observed
she returned to her friends.

The three girls waited for a time by the

spring, thinking they should allow the Blores three quarters of an hour for their dinner, but in less than thirty minutes the ranch house door opened. David and Katherine Blore emerged, carrying a small chest between them.

Instantly Jean and Louise sprang to their feet. They had noted that the couple acted as if afraid someone might observe their strange actions.

"What do you suppose the box contains?" speculated Jean.

"I wish we could find out," Louise returned eagerly. "If it wasn't for our horses——"

By this time the girls noticed that Katherine Blore and her brother intended to carry the box to a shack not far from the ranch house.

"Frances and I will take care of the horses, Louise," Jean offered quickly. "You steal up to the shack and see what you can learn. I have an idea this is important."

Louise did not need to be urged. She quietly walked through the grove, approaching the cabin from the rear. Stealing to a window, she peered inside.

Katherine Blore and her brother had opened the box. As Louise watched in fascination they removed a large quantity of jewels which they sorted into small packets. There were brilliant diamonds, rubies, and green stones which the girl assumed were emeralds.

"Why, they have a fortune in gems!" Louise thought in awe. "They couldn't own them in their own right!"

Instantly it came to her that David Blore and his sister were engaged in a jewel smuggling business. Now it was perfectly clear why the woman had evaded immigration authorities, trying to give out the impression that she had been lost overboard from the *Balaska*. Undoubtedly the Blores had brought their smuggled gems to the ranch to be hidden until they should consider it safe to attempt a sale.

Suddenly a loud droning sound overhead caused Louise to glance up into the sky. A monoplane was circling a nearby field, evidently searching for a smooth landing place.

"It's time I get away from here," the girl told herself. "Otherwise I am likely to be caught!"

She could not resist glancing once more into the shack. Katherine and David Blore, having heard the approaching plane, were trying to finish their task hastily.

"They are expecting someone in that air-plane," Louise thought as she hastened back to the grove.

Quickly she told Jean and Frances what she had seen.

"I wish Uncle Ned were here," she ended with a worried frown. "He would know what to do with these people."

As the girls watched they saw the monoplane make a safe landing not far away. The pilot, a tall, thin man of middle age, came swiftly toward the ranch house. His manner of walking was strangely familiar.

"Ed Newsome!" exclaimed Jean as the newcomer drew closer. "Well, I certainly am surprised."

"This gets more mysterious every minute," commented Louise excitedly.

Katherine and David Blore appeared in the doorway of the shack and greeted the pilot as if he were an old friend. Together the three walked to the ranch house.

"It is as clear as day what they intend to do!" Louise cried in alarm. "The Blores are getting the jewels ready for Newsome to take away in the plane!"

"We must never allow them to succeed!" exclaimed Jean determinedly. "Let's fix the plane so they can't take off!"

"I don't know enough about planes to do it," Louise confessed helplessly.

"I believe I could wreck the ship so it never could take off," Frances offered, as a sudden idea occurred to her.

"How?" asked the Danas together.

"I'll ride my horse over there and make him kick the propeller!"

"Oh, that would be too dangerous," Jean protested quickly. "You might be thrown!"

"I'm not afraid to try it," the girl replied. "I'm a good rider. I'm sure I can manage the horse."

Before the sisters could stop her, Frances sprang into the saddle and cantered away. Courageously she forced her mount close to the plane. As the horse began to buck and kick, Ed Newsome came running from the ranch house.

"Hey! What do you think you are doing?" he shouted furiously.

Louise and Jean were fearful lest their little scheme be revealed, but Frances attempted a very clever act. She pretended that her foot was caught in the stirrup and that she could not free herself or control her mount.

"Good old Frances!" Jean cried approvingly.

The next instant her jubilation turned to horror. The actress's pretense had become reality! As the horse galloped toward the grove she was thrown off and cruelly dragged along.

Now the Dana girls were sorely beset. They must try to help Frances, yet to do so would be to expose themselves to the man and probably lose all chance of proving that the Blores were smugglers.

Fortunately for them Ed Newsome was far more interested in his plane than in the plight of the young horsewoman. Ignoring both rider and animal, he ran toward the field to learn how much damage had been done.

"Now is our chance, Jean!" Louise cried, darting from the trees. "If we work fast we may not be seen!"

CHAPTER XVI

CATTLE RUSTLERS

WHILE Newsome's attention was directed toward his damaged plane, the Dana girls ran from the shelter of trees. Jean caught the runaway horse while Louise quickly freed Frances from the stirrup.

"Are you badly hurt?" she asked anxiously.

"My leg is twisted," the girl answered with a grimace. "The skin is rubbed off my cheek, I guess. It hurts."

"No bones broken?"

"None that I can feel."

"Lean on me," Louise directed as she aided the girl into the grove. "Spare that leg all you can."

"The worst of it is that I'm not sure I damaged the airplane," Frances said with a little moan. "That man came out of the house before I had a chance to do very much."

"Don't worry about that part," declared Jean kindly. "We're happy that you weren't killed. You took a frightful risk."

"Will you be able to ride back to your ranch?" Louise inquired, glancing dubiously at the girl's bruised leg.

"Yes, I think I can make it," Frances replied bravely.

"Then shall we start at once?" Jean suggested uneasily. "Mr. Newsome may decide to investigate, and it will be just as well if he doesn't find us here."

"What about the jewels?" asked Louise.

"We can't stop for anything now," Jean decided. "If we do we'll be caught. Don't you think it would be best to ride back to the ranch and notify the sheriff?"

"Yes," agreed her sister after a moment's thought, "we should be no match for three crooks!"

The girls helped Frances into the saddle again, then quietly rode back to the main highway. So far as they knew they had not been observed by anyone at the Blore ranch.

The trip back required nearly an hour, for Frances Roy's injury was so painful she could not trot nor gallop her horse. She urged Jean and Louise to ride ahead, but they would not desert their friend.

Arriving at the ranch late in the afternoon, Frances was put to bed. A doctor was summoned immediately. Mr. and Mrs. Roy were astounded to learn what had transpired, and the latter telephoned the sheriff's office to ask that a possé of men be sent to investigate the Blores at once.

"I'll get right out there," the man promised. "This sounds serious."

Before the sheriff could start away, another telephone call came into his office. He was told that a group of lawless cattle rustlers had been seen in the vicinity of Red Gulch. Deciding that it was more important to catch the thieves than to make an investigation which might lead to no arrests, the man set out for the hills.

At the Roy ranch Louise and Jean were under the false impression that immediate action was being taken against the Blores. Therefore they made no plans of their own, but assisted their hostess with arrangements for the birthday party which would be held that evening.

The doctor had come and gone. He had treated Frances's injured leg and put healing salve on her face, so that now after a rest she was able to be about.

"If this isn't just my luck," she grumbled as she limped around the house. "Here it is my birthday and I'll not even be able to dance!"

"At least you can eat your share of cake and ice cream," Jean comforted her friend.

The Roys were very popular in the community, and many persons, young and old, had been invited to the party. By seven o'clock cowboys, ranch owners, their wives and daughters, began to arrive. The orchestra struck up and the house rang with laughter.

Louise and Jean were introduced to everyone and never lacked dance partners. Despite her injuries Frances too had a gay time.

Shortly after nine o'clock, when the party was in full swing, Dick Roy heard hoofbeats in the courtyard. A horse galloped up to the door.

"The sheriff has arrived, folks!" the young man called.

"His arm is hanging at his side!" added Glenn. "He has been shot!"

The two boys leaped through the open window and ran to help the sheriff dismount. The guests hurried from the ranch house.

"He must have had a battle with the Blores!" Jean exclaimed to her sister.

The sheriff, hearing the girl's words, shook his head.

"I never got to the Bar II ranch," he told her. "I went after the cattle rustlers but they winged me. They're hiding in the hills south of Red Gulch. I need more men."

At once cowboys ran for their ponies. Soon a large group of riders followed the sheriff away.

"That practically ends our party," sighed Frances, "but we did have a wonderful time while it lasted."

Jean and Louise said very little, although they were worried about the situation at the Blore ranch. They had depended upon the sheriff to make a thorough investigation, and realized now that nothing had been done. With the cowboys and other ranchmen searching for cattle rustlers, they could expect no help from that source. Nor could they ride alone to the Bar II, for their own horses had been borrowed.

"There's nothing we can do except wait until tomorrow," Louise said in disappointment. "It's just a piece of bad luck."

Late that night Glenn and Dick rode back to the ranch to report that the rustlers had not been traced. They gave few details of the search, for the boys, weary from their exhausting ride, went to bed immediately and slept late the following morning.

"We ought not to delay any longer in going to the Blore place," Louise told her sister anxiously.

"Frances isn't able to take us," Jean reminded her sister.

"No, it would be cruel to ask her to ride so far. We'll have to go alone."

The girls saddled their own horses and quietly rode on.

"I hope you know the way," Jean remarked as the girls turned into a narrow trail.

"I didn't pay particular attention, but we should get there all right."

Ultimately the Danas did arrive at their destination, but not before they had experienced a number of harrowing adventures. Twice Louise became confused and took the wrong trail. Once, while she was riding near a herd of grazing cattle, her horse was suddenly attacked by a mad steer. Skillful riding and a cool head saved the girl from disaster. Then, as if they had not had trouble enough, Jean's horse slipped into a deep hole, injuring its leg and causing it to limp.

"Fate seems to be against us today," Louise sighed as the sisters finally came near the Blore ranch house. "I wonder what will happen next?"

Jean was gazing toward the meadow where the Newsome craft had stood.

"I was afraid of that, Louise!" she exclaimed. "The plane is gone!"

"Now what shall we do?"

"Let's ride up boldly to the door and ask Mrs. Blore where Mr. Newsome has taken the ship."

Louise nodded assent, so the girls entered the courtyard and tied their horses to a hitching post. Suddenly old Mrs. Blore appeared. She glanced questioningly at the girls, for she had never seen them before. When Jean explained that they were friends of the Roy family, she seemed to relax.

"We're out for a ride," the girl said.

"Are you all alone today?" Louise inquired casually.

"Yes," murmured the woman sorrowfully. "My son and daughter went away with an unpleasant fellow who came here in a flying machine. I begged them to have nothing to do with him, but they never listen to me."

"Did they mention where they were going?" Jean questioned alertly.

"No, Katherine and David tell me nothing any more. I have worried so much about them that I can't sleep nights—I am practically ill from it."

"Why don't you lie down and rest now?" suggested Louise kindly. "Try to compose your mind. Worry does no good, you know."

"I will try to do as you say. Sleep would make me feel better."

The Dana girls helped the old lady into the house. After she had gone to bed they slipped out of doors once more.

"This is our chance to inspect the shack," Louise proposed eagerly.

"I'll venture to guess the jewels are gone," Jean said gloomily. "Nothing has been going right for us today."

"Even if the Blores did take the gems with them, we might find other evidence which would help to convict them," commented her sister, eager to find any clues to help solve the mystery.

"Yes, we may as well have a look at the place," Jean agreed.

The girls started for the grove, but had gone only a short distance when Louise suddenly pulled her sister behind a clump of bushes.

"Look, Jean!"

Two men whom the girls had never seen before were emerging from the grove. Their faces were grimy, their clothing torn, and they looked as if they might have been hiding in the woods all night. After glancing about carefully and apparently being satisfied that no one was close by, they moved stealthily to the shack and entered it.

"Louise, those men intend to hide there!" Jean whispered to her sister. "Do you know what I think? They are some of the cattle rustlers who eluded the sheriff's posse!"

CHAPTER XVII

HIDDEN IN THE COBWEBS

AFTER a moment of discussion Jean and Louise stole quietly to the shack. As they peered through the rear window, they heard one of the men say:

"This place shore ain't safe, Bill. Ef the sheriff trails us here we'll shore be caught like coyotes in a cloudburst."

"Our best bet's to take fresh hosses an' make fer the canyon," replied the other tersely. "Come on."

Before the Dana girls had time to act, the two men ran across the clearing to their mounts.

"Stop!" shouted Jean angrily. "Don't take our horses!"

Springing into the saddles, the thieves waved their hands arrogantly and rode away.

"Now we are in a nice situation!" Louise said gloomily. "How shall we ever get back to the Roy ranch?"

As the girls discussed their predicament, they heard the quick hoofbeats of approaching horses. The sheriff's possé was coming down the road! A moment later a group of perhaps fifteen men drew rein near Louise and Jean.

136

"We thought the rustlers came this way," shouted the leader. "Haven't seen them, have you?"

"Yes, they stole our horses and rode off," Jean said quickly.

"Straight ahead?"

"Yes, they said they would take to the canyon," offered Louise. "They've not been gone five minutes."

"Ride on, men!" cried the sheriff, spurring his tired horse. "We'll get them yet!"

Mr. Roy, who was a member of the posse, did not follow the others, for he realized that Louise and Jean would have no way of returning to his ranch. After all, they were his guests and young women at that.

"Oh, we feel dreadful about losing your horses," Jean told him contritely.

"It wasn't your fault," answered their host. "I'll probably get them back some time."

He telephoned home and in a short while Glenn and Dick brought extra ponies for the girls. During the ride back to the ranch the Danas told the Roys the details of the disappearance of the Blores.

They agreed with the girls that it would be advisable to send word to their uncle at once. In the afternoon the girls sent off a cable to the *Balaska,* assuring Captain Dana they were positive Miss Blore was alive, although she had disappeared once more.

Frances, who was much improved, rode into town with Louise and Jean in the family car. Later the girls went to the Bar II ranch to deliver a jar of beef broth and other food which Mrs. Roy had prepared for old Mrs. Blore.

"While you give the things to her, Frances," said Louise, "suppose Jean and I wander about outside." As they reached the house she added, "We still want to do a little sleuthing around here."

"Take as long as you wish," replied Frances. "I'll be glad to rest."

The Danas, going directly to the shack, found the place bare of furniture and very dirty. Cobwebs hung in festoons from the ceilings.

The girls were not surprised to discover that the various packets of jewels were no longer there. They could not believe that such a valuable cache would have been left behind by David Blore and his sister.

"My, but this is a spooky place," Jean commented, ruefully brushing a long cobweb from her sleeve. "A regular spider's den."

She glanced at a particularly heavy web in the corner of the room where the Blores previously had been working. Half hidden in the soft, flimsy network was a small scrap of paper.

"Now what is this?" she exclaimed. "Some clue?"

Taking the paper from its nest in the web, she carried it to the window.

"Louise, this is strange," she murmured in a startled voice. "Come here."

Quickly her sister crossed the room to peer over Jean's shoulder. She noticed that the paper bore the insignia of the steamship *Balaska!* Katherine Blore's name was scrawled at the bottom, together with a date which corresponded to the time she had been aboard Captain Dana's vessel.

Even more significant was an itemized list of jewels which read:

> 65 diamonds
> 5 rubies
> 6 emeralds
> 40 pearls

As the rest of the sheet had been torn off, the Danas felt that the list was not complete.

"This is an important clue," Jean declared excitedly. "Why, it practically proves that Miss Blore had the jewels in her possession when she was aboard Uncle Ned's boat!"

"Yes, it does," agreed Louise. "Oh, I don't believe there is a bit of doubt that she and her brother are smugglers!"

"The jewels Miss Blore brought into the country must be worth a fortune! Sixty-five diamonds! Think of that!"

"And we allowed the woman and her brother to get away," Louise said with a groan. "What a fine pair of detectives we are!"

"It wasn't our fault. Everything just conspired against us. Anyway the Blores probably will return here to visit their mother. Then they can be arrested."

"I doubt it, Jean. They have no feeling for her."

"At any rate, this clue in the cobweb should prove of value to the authorities. I'll keep the paper."

Jean carefully folded the slip and placed it in her pocket. Satisfied that the shack held nothing else of interest, the girls returned to the ranch house. Frances met them at the door.

"I am worried about Mrs. Blore," she admitted in a whisper.

"Is she worse?" inquired Louise quickly.

"Yes, she has a fever and talks wildly about her adopted children. I am afraid the poor woman will lose her mind."

The Danas followed their chum into the woman's bedroom, where the old lady sat propped up with pillows. They saw at once that she was not as well as on the previous day.

"How could Katherine and David do such a thing?" she moaned. "I have cared for them since they were babies. Now when I am old and need them most they desert me!"

"Have you learned that they do not intend to return?" Jean inquired as she rearranged the pillows.

"I don't know," the old lady wailed. "They left me no note, no word of explanation when they went."

"Perhaps they were called away for just a few days," Louise said comfortingly, hoping such might be the case.

Both she and Jean felt very sorry for Mrs. Blore, but they believed the old lady would be much better off if she never should see her adopted children again. While the girls were trying to think of something cheerful to say, there was a knock at the door.

"I'll answer it," offered Jean, rather relieved to escape from the bedroom.

"It will be for me," insisted Mrs. Blore, reaching for her bathrobe.

Despite protests from the girls she followed Jean to the door. The visitor was Horace Craven, who smiled broadly as he recognized the Dana girl.

"Well, I had no thought of meeting you again so soon," he said heartily. "Do you live here?"

"No, we came to call," explained Jean, inviting the man into the house. "Mrs. Blore isn't feeling well."

"Oh, I am sorry to hear that," said the diamond merchant. He addressed himself to the old lady. "Perhaps you would prefer that I examine the jewels some other time."

"Jewels?" asked Mrs. Blore blankly.

"Why yes, someone from here sent word to

our firm that you wished a representative to look over a collection of estate gems with a view to their purchase.''

''You must be mistaken. We have no jewels here,'' said the woman firmly.

''This is the Blore ranch, is it not?'' Mr. Craven inquired, deeply puzzled.

''Yes, but I know nothing about any jewels.''

''I am certain—'' The man broke off as he saw that Jean was signaling for him to say no more.

''Oh, Mr. Craven,'' she said significantly, ''you must be very thirsty after your long trip from town. Wouldn't you like something to drink?''

''Thirsty?''

''You really should try the water at the spring,'' added Louise quickly. ''Jean and I will show you where it is.''

''Oh, yes, to be sure,'' the man stammered, for by this time he understood that they wished to get him away from the house.

Leaving Frances with Mrs. Blore, the Dana girls led Mr. Craven a short distance from the dwelling.

''You have something to tell me?'' he questioned, perplexed.

''Yes, about the jewels,'' replied Jean soberly. ''We don't wish Mrs. Blore to hear it, for she has no idea of the truth. We're pretty sure her adopted children, Katherine and David, are smugglers.''

She went on to disclose to the amazed diamond merchant all that she and her sister had discovered in the shack, then showed him the paper which listed the precious stones.

"This is astounding!" he declared after he had read the sheet. "It was David Blore who contacted my firm. And these items tally with the gems he offered for sale."

Mr. Craven assured the girls he would do everything possible to assist in tracing the pair. He promised to notify them at once if he should receive any helpful information.

Presently the three returned to the house where Frances was waiting. After chatting with the man for a few minutes and learning that he had registered at a hotel, she invited him to the Roy ranch to supper.

"I shall be delighted," he accepted gratefully. "It's lonesome staying in a hotel."

When the party arrived at the ranch an hour later, Mrs. Roy greeted the guest cordially. Then she told the girls that she had important news for them.

CHAPTER XVIII

An Attack

"A MESSAGE arrived from Jim Larabee's ranch soon after you girls left," said Mrs. Roy. "It seems they are having a wedding there to-night, and you are all urged to be present. Young Jim is marrying a girl named Betty Brown."

"Why Mother, she is the airplane stewardess I was telling you about!" cried Frances in delight.

"Jim Larabee is a fine man," said Mrs. Roy warmly. "The marriage should be a happy one."

"It will be a wonderful wedding," declared Frances, quickly making plans. "We'll all go, of course. Mr. Craven, you must come with us."

After supper the entire Roy family and their guests drove through the moonlight to the Larabee ranch. Upon their arrival they found many guests ahead of them. The house was beautifully decorated with flowers and ferns. Miss Brown, flushed and excited, had the girls come to her room and talk with her as she dressed.

144

"Isn't this the most un-bridal-like wedding a girl ever had?" she laughed gaily. "No veil, no attendants, not even a new dress. When I decide to do a thing it is always on the spur of the moment!"

"At least you are sparing yourself a great deal of fuss that way," replied Jean, smiling.

"As for your gown, it looks perfectly lovely," added Louise admiringly. "And so do you."

"Thank you very much," replied the smiling bride. "I feel glowing inside and rather tremulous, as if I were walking on clouds!"

Never had the girls attended such a gay, carefree wedding. The ceremony was simple but impressive, and at the proper moment the bridegroom slipped a ring bearing an orange blossom design on Miss Brown's finger.

Afterward refreshments were served, the huge wedding cake was cut, and an orchestra played for dancing. Finally in a shower of confetti the newlyweds departed for an unknown destination, their car bearing white ribbons and a freshly painted sign, "Just Married."

"They will be very happy, I am sure," declared Louise as the automobile disappeared over a hill. "It was a beautiful wedding."

Soon the guests began to leave. As the Dana girls started toward the Roy car they heard an angry shout from the direction of the corral.

"Someone's made off with my hoss!" cried one of the cowboys.

"Mine's gone, too!" came another shout.

A crowd gathered about the two excited young men. At first everyone thought a joke had been played, but it was discovered that two other horses had been left in the places of those taken.

"Strange hosses," said one of the visitors.

"They look like the same horses which were stolen from us at the Blore ranch!" Jean observed as the girls joined the group.

"Yes, they do, Louise! You will recall my horse limped."

Mr. Roy was summoned, and he immediately identified the horses as his property.

"This shore is the work of those rustlers," he declared angrily. "What I can't figure out is why they're roamin' around this particular locality. Why don't they make their get-away?"

"They're up to more mischief, shore as shootin'," drawled one of the men. "How about it, boys? Do we ride 'em down?"

There was a rumble of assent. Immediately the cowboys ran to saddle their mounts. Mr. Roy, weary from a hard day, decided to allow the younger men to take up the search without him. He would ride one of the recovered horses back to his ranch and lead the other. As his wife was invited by a neighbor to go in another car, the young people were left with the Roy automobile.

"Dick, would you mind driving past the Blore ranch?" Jean requested, when they were finally on their way home.

"Why no," he answered instantly. "It's only half a mile farther. Do you think Mrs. Blore may be worse?"

"I feel uneasy about her being there alone," the girl replied. "Especially with rustlers roaming over the countryside."

Some minutes later as the car approached the Blore ranch house, the young people noticed a light burning in one of the windows.

"I imagine everything is all right," remarked Frances.

"Jean, the door of the shack is open!" exclaimed Louise, leaning forward in the car seat.

"We didn't leave it that way!" added her sister.

"No, and I doubt that Mrs. Blore has been well enough to go out of the house."

"Let's investigate," suggested Dick quickly, stopping the car.

Louise and Jean were ahead of the others as everyone jumped from the auto and ran to the shack. Glenn played the bright beam of a flashlight into the room.

"Jean, the cobwebs have been disturbed!" Louise noted at once.

"Yes, they are all torn down!"

"What is so astonishing about that?" inquired Dick in surprise.

"We found a piece of paper—an important clue hidden in the web," Louise explained hurriedly.

"Then it looks as if someone had returned here to search for it," commented Dick thoughtfully.

"Either that, or the person knew about the packet of jewels," replied Jean. "I wonder who it could have been?"

"At any rate the prowler found nothing," declared Louise in satisfaction. "We know the Blores took the jewels with them, and we took the paper."

After closing the door of the building, the young people started toward their car.

"I wonder if we should disturb Mrs. Blore?" Frances asked doubtfully. "It is so late, it might frighten her if we knock on the door."

"I hadn't thought of that," Jean admitted. "But she must have heard the car."

"Listen!" commanded Glenn, stopping suddenly. "What was that?"

"Oh, you're always hearing things," laughed his sister. "I didn't notice anything."

"I thought I heard a plaintive, wailing cry," the young man said.

"It probably was a wild animal or a bird," Frances replied lightly.

As she spoke the sound was repeated. This time everyone heard it.

"The cry came from the house!" exclaimed Jean. "Do you suppose Mrs. Blore can be in trouble?"

With one accord the young people hastened toward the house. Although a light was burning they could not see that anyone was moving about inside. As Dick rapped on the door, the groans became louder.

"This is strange," he said.

"Something is wrong!" Louise cried anxiously. "Mrs. Blore may be very ill!"

Dick tried to open the door only to find it locked.

"Try a window," he urged his brother.

"Locked," reported Glenn.

"Then we shall have to break the glass," Jean said quickly. "We must get in."

Young Roy smashed the pane with a rock, crawled through, and opened the door for the others. The Dana girls were aghast as they entered the living room. Usually so neat and tidy, it was now in great disorder. Furniture had been upset and broken, desk drawers emptied. Even a few floor boards had been pried up.

"What has happened here?" gasped Frances in dismay. "Where is Mrs. Blore?"

A low moan of pain drew the group to her bedroom. On the floor lay the old woman, her hands scratched and bruised, blood oozing from a head wound.

Lifting her gently, the young people placed her on the bed. As they did so she winced with pain, crying out.

"Who did this to you?" demanded Louise. "Tell us what happened."

"Two—men," murmured Mrs. Blore brokenly. "They beat me—because I had no jewels!"

A convulsive shudder wracked the thin body. The victim's head fell back on the pillow and she lay still.

CHAPTER XIX

A BLACK BOX

"MRS. BLORE isn't dead, is she?" Frances whispered in horror. "Oh, this is dreadful."

"No, she is sleeping," Louise replied, bending over the old lady. "She must have gone through a terrible ordeal. It has left her completely exhausted."

"I never thought anyone would be vicious enough to attack a helpless old lady!" Frances declared indignantly. "Who could it have been?"

"Evidently someone who knew that Katherine and David Blore had jewels in their possession," Louise said thoughtfully.

"I wish Mrs. Blore had told us just what happened before she dropped off to sleep," commented Jean, frowning.

"How about a doctor?" inquired Glenn quietly. "Dick and I better go to town for one."

"I wish you would," Louise replied with a grateful smile. "And it might be well to bring a nurse, too. I doubt that Mrs. Blore will be able to get out of bed for many days."

After Glenn and Dick had driven away, the Dana girls heated water and sponged Mrs. Blore's face and hands. While they were working over her, she opened her eyes again.

"Water, please," she whispered.

Frances ran to get a glassful from the kitchen.

"Are you able to tell us now what happened?" Louise asked gently after the woman had sipped a little of the water. "Who were the men who beat you so cruelly?"

"I never saw them before," Mrs. Blore answered hoarsely.

"Were they rough looking men?" questioned Jean. "Like rustlers?"

"Yes, their clothes were muddy and torn. They acted desperate."

"Were they about the same height?" asked Louise, an idea in her mind.

"Very nearly. One might have been a few inches taller than the other."

"Were they riding?"

"Yes. That was what deceived me. I heard the horses and thought they belonged to Jake Glossman. So foolishly I opened the door."

"Jake Glossman's horses were stolen tonight from the Larabee ranch," Frances declared in a startled voice.

From the first Louise and Jean had held the opinion that Mrs. Blore had been attacked by the cattle rustlers. Her description of the men confirmed their suspicion.

"What did they say to you?" Jean asked the old lady.

"As soon as I opened the door they forced their way into the house," she replied. "They demanded jewels. When I said I had none they told me I lied. They struck me and tried to make me tell where I had hidden them."

"Those men will be caught and punished!" Frances declared feelingly. "Don't you worry about that part, Mrs. Blore."

"I couldn't make them believe I had no money or jewels. They upset everything in the house and even tore up the floor boards. Then they knocked me down so hard, I couldn't get up."

"Try not to think about it any more," Louise said kindly. "Just lie still and rest."

"I ache in every bone of my body," Mrs. Blore moaned. "First my children desert me, and now this trouble! It is too much to bear." She started to weep.

"You have had more than your share of bad luck," Jean agreed, starting to carry the wash basin back to the kitchen. "But everything will come out all right."

As she emptied the water into the sink, she decided that while Louise and Frances remained with Mrs. Blore, she would try to straighten up the disordered house. After setting the living room to rights she entered an adjoining den.

Here the contents of the desk had been scat-

tered helter-skelter over the floor. As the girl
began to pick up the letters and papers she
observed that a small black box had been upset.
Its lid had fallen off, and a white powder it con-
tained had spilled on the rug.

Picking up the box, Jean wondered what the
contents were. The powder had a faint odor
which seemed vaguely familiar.

"I ought to brush up this stuff before it gets
ground into the rug," she told herself.

She started toward the kitchen intending to
look for a whisk broom and dust pan. Before
she had taken a dozen steps, she became aware
of a dizzy feeling. As the girl grasped the arm
of a chair for support, her head began to whirl.
Then she became very drowsy.

"Louise!" she called in a weak voice.
"Louise!" In another second she had slumped
into a chair and fallen into a deep slumber.

Hearing her voice called, the older Dana girl
left Frances with Mrs. Blore and hastened to
the den, where she saw Jean lying asleep in a
chair. She was deeply puzzled.

"Did you call me?" she asked, giving her
sister a little shake. "What's the matter?"

Jean did not stir.

"This is queer," Louise thought in perplexity. "I was positive she called my name."

She tried again to arouse Jean, and failing,
realized that the girl's sleep was too sound to
be natural.

"Why, she acts just as Mr. Wharton did when he was drugged!" Louise reflected with growing alarm.

As her gaze roved slowly about the room, she noticed the black box and the white powder scattered on the rug. A faint odor lingered in the air. Instantly the conviction came to Louise that Jean had been overpowered by the scent. In some way the white powder had produced the trance-like condition.

Going to the kitchen Louise dampened a towel, which she placed over her nose and mouth as a mask. Then she returned to the den, hastily scooped up the powder and dumped it into the box.

"I'll keep this and have a chemical analysis made," she decided, slipping it into her pocket.

After opening all the windows, Louise tried once more to awaken her sister.

"Probably the best thing to do is just let her sleep," the girl told herself. "She ought to come out of it soon."

For the next hour Louise divided her time between Mrs. Blore and her sister. She did not tell Frances of her fears, but allowed her to believe that Jean had fallen asleep because of exhaustion.

Shortly before midnight Glenn and Dick returned with a doctor and a nurse. The sound of the automobile seemed to arouse Jean, who stirred, yawned and sat up.

"Gracious, where am I?" she asked, looking about in a dazed way.

"Don't you remember anything?" Louise questioned her sister.

"We were at the Blore ranch, weren't we?" asked Jean slowly.

"We still are," Louise answered dryly. "Why did you come into this den?"

"I intended to straighten it up."

"Do you remember noticing a box of white powder on the floor?"

"Why, yes, now that you remind me, I do. I was going to brush it up. I guess I must have dropped off to sleep."

"You have been sleeping for nearly two hours, Jean. How do you feel?"

"A little light-headed."

"Exactly the way I felt after I fell asleep at the Wharton house!" Louise cried triumphantly. "Jean, you must have breathed fumes from the powder and it put you to sleep!"

"Do you suppose that *was* what happened?"

"I am positive of it, Jean."

"How did the powder get here?"

"The Blores may have had it at the Wharton house and brought some of it here. Perhaps when they fled so hastily they left it behind without meaning to."

"A sleep-producing powder would be very useful to them in case they were ever surprised by officers," Jean remarked slowly.

"Certainly. One whiff of the powder and their enemies would go off to dreamland while they made good their escape."

"Let's not tell anyone about this," Jean said hastily as the Roy brothers brought the doctor and the nurse into the house. "Does Frances suspect?"

"No, she merely thought you were worn out from the party," Louise replied in a low tone, "and fell asleep naturally."

Doctor Keswick was a stout, dignified-looking man who wasted few words. He was very cheerful in Mrs. Blore's presence, but after he had examined the woman, he drew the Dana girls aside to tell them his verdict.

"Mrs. Blore will recover from her bruises," he said quietly, "but she has a very serious heart murmur. While she may live for years under good care, I doubt that she ever will be well again."

"Is there nothing that can be done?" asked Louise.

"Rest, absolute freedom from worry, and good care, will prolong her life. Medicine will be of slight value."

"I see," said Jean soberly. "Unfortunately Mrs. Blore is inclined to worry a great deal, especially about her adopted children."

"It might be advisable to send for them if they are away," the physician suggested.

Louise shook her head. "That is impossible,

Doctor Keswick. In any case, I doubt if they would come even though word might reach them.''

With a capable nurse in charge there was no longer any reason for the young people to remain. Before returning to the Roy ranch, Frances promised the sick woman that the next morning she would have her mother locate a housekeeper to come when she was better.

It was well after one o'clock when the Roy car reached home. Lights glowed in the ranch house, and Frances wondered if her parents had become alarmed over the long absence of the young people.

However, as they alighted from the automobile they observed that a number of cowboys had gathered near a barn. Several horses were tied near by.

''Say, I believe they've caught the cattle rustlers!'' Dick shouted, as he started for the group on a run.

The others followed. By the light of lanterns they saw the two cattle thieves, their hands bound behind them, being marched to a waiting car. The girls were told it would take the men to the county jail. Mr. Roy revealed that the fellows had been captured in a ravine after a brief exchange of rifle fire.

''Oh, Jean, I wish we could question the rustlers before they are locked up!'' Louise exclaimed impulsively.

"No reason why you can't," the rancher assured her. "Go ahead."

Before talking with the two prisoners, Jean and Louise, supported in their story by Frances and her brothers, told Mr. Roy of the brutal beating which Mrs. Blore had received. The young people felt that these men answered the description provided by the old lady.

"We ain't never been near the Bar II ranch in all our lives," one of the outlaws denied sullenly when confronted with a direct accusation.

"We have proof you were there once," retorted Jean coolly, "for you stole our horses. It will be very easy to have Mrs. Blore identify you both."

"We also saw you enter the shack," added Louise severely. "Was that where you learned about the hidden jewels?"

"We don't know nothin' about any jewels."

"I am sure you did not find them," Louise went on smoothly. "They are in the hands of persons even worse than yourselves."

"You mean that fellow Newsome?"

"So you know him?" asked Louise.

"We heard him talkin' with the Blores," the rustler muttered sullenly.

"So that was how you really learned about the jewels!" Jean exclaimed.

"I'd like to see him in jail!" the outlaw growled.

"We agree in that matter," replied Louise.

"If Mr. Newsome can be traced he will be arrested."

"Say, maybe we could give you a tip where to find him," the man suggested slyly. "That is, if you'll let us off."

"I'd like to hear your story," Louise replied, trying not to appear too eager. "I'm afraid I have nothing to say about the other."

"I don't know the state where Newsome went," answered the outlaw, "but it's somewhere in the East." The girl wondered if the man would tell anything more. Apparently he decided not to dicker about his release, for he added, "Me and my pal heard him say he was flyin' back to a city called Penfield."

CHAPTER XX

The Crown Jewels

THE announcement of the cattle rustler that Ed Newsome had returned to Penfield filled Louise and Jean with secret elation. They might have an opportunity yet to track down the man and his dishonest associates, Katherine and David Blore!

Although the girls asked the man many more questions they learned nothing further of interest. Presently the cowboys took the prisoners into town and turned them over to the sheriff.

The following morning Louise, Jean and Frances regretfully said farewell to everyone on the ranch. Their brief vacation over, they must return to Starhurst School.

"I don't mind the thought as much as I did since we've learned Ed Newsome may be at Penfield," Jean declared with a sigh. "But even so, I hate to go."

"We've never had a more thrilling vacation," Louise added. "So much has been packed into a few days."

"I hope Mrs. Blore gets along well," remarked Frances anxiously.   "She's really a nice old lady."

"I will see that she has a good housekeeper," Mrs. Roy promised.   "As often as possible I'll run over there to be sure she's being taken care of properly."

Mr. Roy took the girls to the airport to catch the one o'clock plane back to Penfield.

"You should be at Starhurst School in time for Monday morning classes," he told them as final good-byes were said.   "Send me a wire, Frances, as soon as you arrive."

"I shall, Dad."

"We've had a perfectly wonderful time," Louise declared, clasping the rancher's hand.

"Yes indeed," added Jean heartily.   "We'll remember this vacation always."

Soon after the girls had taken their seats in the plane, it made a smooth take-off from the field.

"We'll miss Betty Brown," Frances remarked as they settled themselves for the long journey East.

The novelty of flying over changing scenes intrigued the girls, with the beauty of colorful clouds still the most interesting.   They had not been in the air three hours when Louise called attention to the fact that they were running into heavy fog.   Wisps of smoke-like vapor curled about the wing-tips.

Soon a red light flashed a signal to the stewardess. She went forward to talk with the pilot, returning to tell the passengers that a landing must be made.

"The fog is much worse ahead," the young woman explained. "It seems advisable to drop down at Coltertown where there is an emergency landing field."

Although recognizing the wisdom of the pilot's decision, the girls were disappointed at the delay. Unless the fog should clear away very soon they would be late in arriving at Penfield.

"I'm afraid Mrs. Crandall will not listen to our excuses, either," sighed Frances. "She will say we should have taken an earlier plane."

Coltertown proved to be a small place of less than eight hundred inhabitants. A taxi was provided to take the passengers to a nearby hotel, but Frances and the Dana girls elected to remain at the field with the stewardess, pilot, and co-pilot.

To pass the time the group lunched together at a restaurant across the road from the hangars. When the conversation turned to hobbies, the pilot remarked that he was deeply interested in music; in fact, could play several instruments.

"Then you should hear about my sister's invention," Louise declared mischievously.

To Jean's embarrassment her sister described the machine in detail, even drawing a diagram of the interesting gadget.

"That sounds to me like a good idea," the man said seriously.

"There is only one thing the matter with the machine," Jean sighed. "I can't make it work!"

At the time the pilot said no more, but after Louise and the stewardess had gone away together he encouraged Jean to talk more about her invention.

"I wish I might see your invention," he remarked regretfully. "I know a good bit about machinery, and from your description it strikes me you may be using the wrong type of gears."

After Jean had asked many eager questions, the young man wrote down the name of a place where he thought she could get the type of gears required.

"Let me know if you are successful," he requested as they left the restaurant together. "I might be your first customer for a machine!"

"What would you do with it?" Jean inquired, smiling. "You don't have much time for your music, do you?"

"I compose music in my spare moments," the man laughed. "Unfortunately it takes too long to write it all down, so often I lose my best compositions. Your invention would solve my difficulties—as well as other people's."

The fog showed no indication of lifting. As Jean and the pilot stood gazing across the runway, the field emergency lights flashed on, flooding the ground as sunshine would.

"What plane is that coming in?" she inquired, hearing the roar of its motors.

"It must be No. 736 on the TLA line. Pilot McKensey probably has been grounded too."

The huge transport made a successful landing and taxied to the hangar. As Jean watched the passengers alight, she suddenly saw a familiar face.

"Mr. Craven!" she exclaimed, rushing forward to grasp the man's hand. "We meet again!"

"Well, well, this is a pleasure," he said heartily. "It very nearly makes the fog worth while. You are not traveling alone?"

"No, Louise and Frances are somewhere around," the girl replied.

"I have rather important news which might interest you and your sister," Mr. Craven said soberly. "Where may we talk privately?"

"I'm afraid there's no place here. We might walk a bit. My sister is in the waiting room. I'll get her."

In a moment Jean returned with Louise who was delighted to see the diamond merchant again. The three moved some distance away from the other passengers.

"Have you received information about Katherine and David Blore?'' Louise inquired eagerly, hoping the man might have a clue for them.

Mr. Craven shook his head.

"No, I'm sorry to say. What I heard may have no bearing upon the case, either, yet I feel it is significant. Just before boarding the plane for New York I received a wire telling me that dealers have been warned to be on their guard against buying jewels which may have been stolen from a crown piece formerly on display at a European museum.''

"Did you learn when the crown disappeared?'' Louise asked thoughtfully.

"At approximately the time Katherine Blore sailed on your uncle's ship.''

"Then you think——?''

"Oh, I venture no opinion, Louise,'' the diamond merchant said hastily. "I merely pass the information on to you for what it may be worth. There may be no connection.''

"Did you get a list of the stolen jewels?'' questioned Jean, wondering if it would correspond with the one they had found in the shack at the Bar II ranch.

"I have wired a request for it, but as yet have not received it.''

Mr. Craven noted down the Penfield address of the Dana girls, promising to notify them if he should obtain more detailed information regarding the stolen crown jewels.

"We certainly hope you do," said Jean excitedly.

Two additional hours were spent at the air field, but at dusk the fog lifted slightly. With clear weather reported ahead, the two planes took off once more for the East. Frances and the Dana girls did not reach Starhurst School in time for Monday morning classes. As they confidently expected, Mrs. Crandall called them to her office to give a lecture for the late return.

"I understand that weather is quite beyond one's control," she commented after hearing their explanation. "In a way it could not be helped, I suppose, yet you should have taken an earlier plane, thus allowing yourself a margin of safety. The influence of extended absences has a bad effect on other students who return from vacations on time."

"You are right, of course, Mrs. Crandall," agreed Frances and the Danas meekly. The subject was dropped by the headmistress.

Jean had worried about her invention during the vacation period, fearing that it might have been stolen or damaged. She was relieved when Evelyn Starr, who had guarded it for her, returned the machine in perfect condition. Laughingly the girl remarked that even Lettie Briggs did not know its hiding place!

Every moment she could spare from her studies Jean spent working on her "brain child." Recalling what the airplane pilot had told her about gears, she installed a new set, using a more complicated arrangement.

Then came an afternoon when she fingered "Old Black Joe" on the keyboard. To her delight she discovered that save for a few notes the composition had recorded perfectly on the roll of paper in the machine!

"Louise, I've done it!" she cried triumphantly. "At last my machine works!"

When her sister came to view the miracle, she too became excited. The news spread over the dormitory, and many who had laughed at Jean now declared warmly that "they always knew she could do it."

Lettie Briggs and Ina Mason took no pleasure in Jean's success. They refused to believe the machine would work until they saw for themselves how it recorded any selection that was played on the piano keys.

"I'm sure it isn't much good," Lettie said scoffingly to the young inventor. "It keeps making mistakes when it records. It's just a silly idea."

"I know why it does that," Jean returned, untroubled. "I can fix it so it will operate perfectly within a few days."

"Perhaps I'll do a little fixing of my own," Lettie muttered under her breath. Those in the room did not hear her.

The troublesome girl brooded over Jean's good fortune until she could not bear the thought another instant. As she went downstairs to get the morning mail the following day she turned over various plans in her mind. As there were no letters for her, Lettie soon started back to her room. One of the teachers stopped her.

"Oh, Lettie, will you please tell Louise and Jean Dana that a special delivery letter has just arrived for them? They will have to sign for it in the office."

"I'll send them right down," Lettie replied quickly, as an evil idea came into her mind.

Going directly to the suite occupied by the girls, she gave them the message. Having no suspicion of the malicious thoughts harbored by Lettie, Jean and Louise ran downstairs to sign for the letter. In their haste they did not bother to lock the door.

"Now is my chance!" Lettie told herself grimly. "The chance I've been waiting for."

Jean's invention had been left on the table in plain sight. Crossing over to it quickly the girl hesitated a moment, then deliberately pushed the machine off the table. It struck the floor with a loud crash. Instantly several wires snapped and a piece which broke off rolled across the floor.

"Oh!" the girl gasped.

For an instant Lettie was frightened and her face became pale. She had not intended to do as much damage to the invention as now seemed apparent. In another moment her worry vanished.

"What do I care?" she said to herself as she hurried to her own room. "Serves Jean Dana right for acting so smart all the time!"

CHAPTER XXI

DISASTER FOR JEAN

BEFORE returning to their room, the Dana
girls decided to open the special delivery letter.
Delighted to learn that it came from Horace
Craven, they could hardly wait to read it.

"What does he say?" Jean asked eagerly,
peering over her sister's shoulder. "Has he
discovered anything new about Katherine
Blore?"

"Listen to this!" Louise replied. "You remember at the Roy ranch we gave Mr. Craven
a description of Miss Blore. Well, he says he
cabled it to Europe and it appears that a woman
who closely resembles her was seen loitering
at the museum shortly before the crown jewels
were stolen!"

"Then it is practically certain she was the
person who took the crown and smuggled it
into this country!" cried Jean.

"Yes, Mr. Craven says a general alarm has
been sent out for her arrest."

"Oh, I hope the authorities catch her," Jean
murmured as she read the letter herself.

The girls discussed the communication for

171

some time, then returned to their room. Opening the door, Jean gasped in dismay. Her precious music recording machine was lying on its side on the floor.

"Louise, my invention!"

"Oh, Jean, how could you have been so careless? It must have tumbled off the table. You probably set it too close to the edge."

"I didn't," protested Jean, fighting back the tears. "I distinctly remember leaving it in the very center of the table."

"Perhaps it hasn't been damaged," Louise said hopefully. "Let's look."

A hasty examination disclosed not only that the machine would not operate, but that it was almost ruined.

"Several wires have broken, the gears are jammed, and a piece is gone," Jean reported with a groan. "I can't tell how much more damage has been done. Who could have done such a mean thing?"

"You are convinced the machine was wrecked deliberately?" Louise asked.

"Of course. It never could have fallen from the table by itself."

"Lettie gave us the message about the special delivery letter. I wonder——"

"She has been jealous of me ever since I started to build the machine!" Jean cried indignantly. "I think I shall report her to Mrs. Crandall."

"We have no proof she did it," Louise returned quietly.

"Oh, I am certain she did it!"

"If I were you I should say nothing about it. Can you rebuild the machine?"

"Probably, but it will take me a long while," said Jean sadly. "Oh, I'm sick over this. I had counted upon having it ready for a demonstration by the fourteenth when we give our school concert."

"I'll help you all I can, Jean," replied her sister sympathetically.

"Before I start work I must go to Penfield and buy new parts."

"Find out what you need, Jean, and we'll leave at once. We might stop in to see Wu Sing while we are there."

Telling no one of the disaster, the girls got permission to go to town and caught a bus into Penfield. After Jean had made her purchases they called at the laundry of Wu Sing. They were elated to learn that during their absence in the West the laundryman had succeeded in tracing Charlie Young. He knew where the man was hiding, and promised that if the girls would return the following day he would have him at the shop to talk with them.

"We really should call upon the MacVey family, too," Louise remarked as the sisters left the laundry. "I hope they have had no more trouble since we left."

"When we go, let's take the little black box along with us and show it to Mrs. MacVey," Jean suggested thoughtfully. "I wish we could have the powder analyzed and learn if it really does produce sleep."

"You might test it out yourself," Louise proposed with a laugh.

"No, thank you! If I am to get my music recording machine repaired before the concert I can't afford to waste any time in unrequired sleep!"

Upon arriving at the dormitory the two girls set to work upon the invention. Fortunately the damage was not as great as Jean had thought, but it required long and tedious hours to substitute new parts for those broken. Throughout the evening the Dana girls toiled, keeping their door locked, and ignoring all knocks.

Just before the "lights out" signal, the last bolt was screwed into place on the machine and a test satisfied Jean that the gadget worked even better than before.

"It doesn't seem to make a single mistake now in recording the music!" she cried in delight. "Oh, Louise, I believe Lettie did me a real favor, although she had no intention of doing so!"

"I wish you would get the machine patented before anything happens to it again, Jean."

"Tomorrow I'll show it to Mr. Crandall. If

he thinks the machine is valuable, I'll ask him to take the steps necessary to protect the invention.''

"That's a good idea," said her sister.

The next morning Jean made an appointment with the husband of the headmistress to give him a demonstration of what her invention would do. She remained with him an hour, then left the office, flushed with happiness at his high praise.

"What did he say?" Louise asked anxiously.

"Mr. Crandall seemed very excited over the invention. He complimented me a great deal, and promised to take care of having it patented. As soon as I have protection, it will be demonstrated to the entire school!"

"Oh, I am so proud of you, Jean," Louise declared, giving her sister an affectionate squeeze.

"I never could have finished the machine if you hadn't encouraged me and helped me," Jean replied loyally.

In the school concert, to be given the following evening, both Dana girls were to take leading parts. After a long and tiring rehearsal they hurriedly departed for Wu Sing's laundry to keep their appointment with him.

"We have so many things to do these days, it's just rush, rush, rush," Jean said with a sigh. "My poor mind is a whirl of concerts, classes, machines——"

"Sleeping powders, smuggling and China-men," finished Louise with a chuckle.

The girls reached the laundry a few minutes late. Charlie Young, having arrived ahead of them, was pacing the floor nervously.

"Charlie think maybe Missees not come," he sighed in relief.

The change in the man's appearance was startling. He had lost weight, his face was drawn and tired looking, and his clothes were wrinkled and torn.

"Charlie, please tell us exactly what happened to you," urged Jean. "Was it Mr. Newsome who took you away in his car?"

"Yes," replied the young man. "Newsome carry me in auto-car to river. Then take me to shack on island. Keep me prisoner long time, hands bound, handkerchief-gag over mouth. Charlie be there yet maybe, only boys peep in window, see Charlie, set him free."

"Have you any idea why you were held a prisoner?" questioned Louise.

"Charlie think Missee Blore and no-good brother order it so. Charlie know too much."

"You mean in regard to their smuggling activities?" Jean asked.

The Chinese gave the girl a quick, appraising glance.

"Know nothing about smuggling," he replied briefly. "Know nothing."

"At any time did you see jewels in the possession of the Blores?"

"Missee Blore have sparkle-glass necklace," the Chinaman answered evasively. "Velly cheap, Charlie think."

"No, I mean unmounted stones," Jean told him. "Rubies, emeralds and diamonds, alone, not in rings."

Charlie hesitated, obviously afraid to reveal his knowledge.

"We are your friends," Louise said quietly.

"Charlie see jewels in house after Missee come back from tlip over water. No-good brother think Charlie run to police. So he tell Newsome man keep Charlie prisoner while they make get-away quick."

"When did you first meet Ed Newsome?" inquired Jean.

Charlie Young glanced at Wu Sing and did not speak.

"Better you tell all," Wu Sing said after a moment of silence. "These girls our friends. Maybe they help us."

At Jean's repeated urging Charlie revealed what the girls had suspected for some time. Newsome had aided both Wu Sing and his friend to enter the country illegally. Although they had paid the man well, he had never been satisfied, and came to them with repeated demands for money.

"Newsome work same racket-game on other China boys," Charlie Young disclosed. "Missees not tell this to anyone!"

As Jean and Louise did not reply, a look of fear came into the young Oriental's eyes.

"Missees please give promise?" he pleaded anxiously. "Charlie die velly quick in jail-house."

"You'll not be sent to jail," Louise assured him, "but I suppose the immigration authorities could deport you both."

"Much better die than go back to China," Charlie said dismally. "I want stay here."

"We'll do the very best we can for you," Jean promised, as the girls turned to leave. "You can't go on as you have in the past, paying tribute to Ed Newsome and being in constant fear of arrest."

Enroute to Starhurst School she and Louise talked over the situation. They both liked Charlie Young and Wu Sing and felt very sorry for the Orientals. However, they had committed a serious offence, and clearly it was the girls' duty as citizens to report them to the authorities.

"If we don't tell, Newsome may escape punishment," Jean declared miserably. "And if we do tell, Charlie and Wu Sing are almost certain to be deported. What a predicament we are faced with!"

"We need the advice of an older person, Jean," Louise decided.

"Suppose we consult Mr. and Mrs. Crandall," her sister suggested.

"An excellent idea," approved Louise instantly. "Let's go to their office just as soon as we reach the school."

"I hope everything will come out all right," said Jean. "I'm getting a bit fearful, the whole thing is such a mess."

"That's true," agreed Louise. "On the other hand, we've had so many clues the past few days I have a feeling the mystery will be solved soon!"

CHAPTER XXII

A PERPLEXING PROBLEM

UPON arriving at the Starhurst School, the Danas went directly to the office only to learn that Mr. and Mrs. Crandall were too busy arranging last-minute concert details to see anyone until the next day.

"I suggest you return in the morning at nine o'clock," they were advised by the secretary.

"Very well. Will you please make an appointment for that hour?" requested Louise politely.

The girls had been so occupied with other affairs they had given little thought to the coming concert. However, they knew their parts well and were not afraid of failure.

"I hope everything goes off fine tonight," Jean remarked as the sisters dressed for the performance. "Somehow I don't trust Lettie."

"That's not surprising after the way she tried to ruin your music machine," returned Louise dryly. "Do you know, I suspect Mrs. Crandall has an inkling of the truth."

"What makes you think so? I never told her anything about it," said Jean.

180

"Our headmistress has a way of learning things. I wonder how Lettie feels after planning on being in the concert tonight."

"She had her heart set upon doing a solo part, I was told."

"And then suddenly to have her name withdrawn and another girl's substituted!"

"That was peculiar, wasn't it?" Jean admitted thoughtfully. "Mrs. Crandall never does anything without a good reason."

"Lettie has been blaming us because she isn't to be in the concert."

"Yes, I know. That is why I am afraid she may try one of her little tricks tonight, Louise."

"I don't see what she can do. Your invention is quite safe?"

"Mr. Crandall has it locked in his office," replied Jean. "It ought to be safe there."

"Then I see no reason to worry."

The girls had just finished dressing when Evelyn Starr came to the door to give them a message from the office.

"How lovely you both look," she said admiringly. "Mrs. Crandall wishes you to come downstairs at once if you can."

"She must have decided to talk with us after all," Louise commented in surprise. "But this is an odd time to grant an interview. It's nearly the concert hour."

"I think you have a visitor," Evelyn explained. "As least I saw a tall, distinguished looking man with a dark moustache talking with the headmistress."

"We don't know anyone who fits that description, do we, Louise?" Jean asked in perplexity.

"No, I'm sure I have no idea who it could be," agreed her sister.

"Why not run down and find out?" suggested Evelyn with an amused laugh. "He really is handsome."

As the Dana girls entered the office, they were astonished to see Mr. Craven, and with him a dark stranger who had aroused Evelyn's admiration. The gentleman was introduced as Frank Fleetwood.

"Not Frank Fleetwood, the well-known detective?" Jean inquired in awe.

"I have had some good luck in solving smuggling cases," the man admitted carelessly.

"Mr. Fleetwood is investigating the crown jewel theft," Mr. Craven told the girls quickly. "I brought him here to talk over the Blore-Newsome affair. I thought you could give him first-hand information which might be useful."

"We'll be glad to help in any possible way," Jean replied, glancing uneasily at the clock on a side wall.

"I hope we are not keeping you from an engagement," Mr. Craven said, noticing that the girls were dressed in evening gowns.

"The school is giving a concert," explained Louise. "Jean and I are taking part and the program is scheduled to start in ten minutes."

"Then we have arrived at an inopportune moment. If Mrs. Crandall has no objection, suppose Mr. Fleetwood and I wait here in the office until after the performance?"

"That would be over an hour," said Louise.

Jean suggested that time might pass more enjoyably for the visitors if they should attend the concert. Arrangements were made with the headmistress, then the Danas escorted the men to the auditorium as their guests.

Lettie Briggs chanced to meet the group at the main doorway. She deliberately paused, compelling the girls to introduce her. To their embarrassment she tried to make an impression upon Mr. Fleetwood.

The detective, smiling tolerantly, said very little. However, after Lettie had entered the auditorium, Mr. Craven mentioned that he once had had some experience with the girl's parents.

"Mr. and Mrs. Briggs are very wealthy," he said, "but they drive a hard bargain."

After Mr. Craven and the detective had found seats, Jean and Louise hastened backstage. To their surprise they discovered Lettie awaiting them.

"Why, Lettie, only persons who are in the concert are supposed to be here," Jean said in quick protest.

"No one will notice me unless you start shouting about it! I just came back for a moment to ask you about Mr. Fleetwood. He's very handsome!''

"Yes, he is," agreed Jean with an amused smile. "But a good bit older than we are."

"Is he a special friend of yours?"

"We haven't time to tell you about him now," answered Jean impatiently. "It's nearly eight o'clock and we must be on the stage."

She and Louise opened a door which entered upon the stairway to the stage. As they passed through, they turned their backs upon Lettie. Infuriated, the girl deliberately slammed the door so that it caught the skirt of Louise's long evening gown, which ripped as she took a step forward.

"Oh, now what shall I do!" Louise exclaimed in dismay as she saw the damage which had been done. "My dress is ruined! I can never appear on the stage!"

Jean jerked open the door and looked about for Lettie. The girl had fled.

"If that isn't the meanest trick yet!" she cried indignantly.

"I can't be in the concert now," Louise repeated, close to tears. "My dress is a sight."

"Let me see what I can do with it."

Assisted by Evelyn Starr who came by just at that moment, Jean pinned the dress so that the tear was not noticeable.

"There, no one will ever see the rip," she

declared, surveying her work. "Just be careful."

The girls barely had time to take their places on the stage when the curtain went up. The program was given without a flaw. One number in particular, a soprano solo by Frances Roy, received rounds of applause. As an encore she sang a Western song which Louise and Jean knew well. At a signal from their chum they joined in the second chorus, adding to the effectiveness of the number.

During a brief intermission the Dana girls rejoined Mr. Craven and Mr. Fleetwood, taking Frances with them. From a seat at the rear of the auditorium Lettie Briggs watched jealously as the Western girl was introduced to the detective. Upon learning that she lived near the Blore ranch Mr. Fleetwood displayed a special interest, but before he could ask any questions, it was time for the concert to be resumed and the girls had to leave.

According to plan the program should have ended at ten-thirty, but the large number of encores carried it on much later. When the final number had been played, it was nearly half past eleven. Without stopping to receive the congratulations of their friends, Jean and Louise hastened to meet Mr. Craven and the detective.

"You have waited a long while," Louise said apologetically.

"Oh, we enjoyed the concert," the diamond merchant responded. "The time has passed swiftly."

Before they could leave the auditorium, Mrs. Crandall came to speak with the two men.

"I had no idea the concert would last so long," she declared regretfully. "I am sorry to disappoint you, but I really feel it is too late for you to talk with Louise and Jean this evening. Would it be possible for you to return in the morning?"

"Why, yes, I can call then," replied Mr. Fleetwood with only a slight hesitation. "Mr. Craven and I had intended to take rooms at the hotel. Our train does not leave Penfield until after ten o'clock tomorrow."

"Then perhaps you could see the girls early in the morning," Mrs. Crandall suggested. "If necessary I can arrange to have them excused from their first class."

It was definitely decided that Louise and Jean should meet the men in the downstairs reception room at eight o'clock. Mr. Craven and the detective then departed, apparently not in the least annoyed because they had been unable to obtain the interview.

"I wish Mrs. Crandall hadn't been so strict," Jean declared as the girls returned to their suite. "But there will be one advantage in postponing the call to tomorrow."

"Meaning that we may get out of a class?"

"Yes," laughed Jean. She carefully wound the clock and set it for an early morning hour. "We have been so busy today I forgot about writing a required English theme. So you see, a prolonged interview will be exactly to my liking!"

CHAPTER XXIII

THE WATER WHEEL

PROMPTLY at eight o'clock the following morning Mr. Craven and the detective presented themselves at Starhurst School. Louise and Jean had no difficulty in extending the interview far past nine o'clock, for they had a great deal to tell the men.

After relating all the facts they had gathered about Katherine and David Blore and the cache of jewelry, the girls cautiously mentioned the two Chinese, Charlie Young and Wu Sing. Receiving a promise that the Orientals would not be arrested until an extensive investigation had been made, they expressed their belief that Ed Newsome had forced the two foreigners to pay extortion money.

"I will talk with Wu Sing immediately," promised Mr. Fleetwood. "Would you girls like to accompany me to the laundry?"

"Yes indeed," Louise accepted quickly, "if Mrs. Crandall will allow us to leave the school."

When the matter was explained to the headmistress, she decided that the girls might be excused from their morning classes. A taxi carried the party to Wu Sing's shop in Penfield. Alighting, Louise and Jean noticed at once that the place had a deserted appearance. Blinds were drawn, and a freshly painted sign in Chinese and English had been tacked to the door.

"What does it say?" Jean asked with misgiving as they reached the door.

"Customers are supposed to call for their laundry at the Lee Wong shop on Clark Street," Louise interpreted, slowly making out the queerly worded message.

"That means your friend Wu Sing has taken himself to parts unknown," observed Mr. Fleetwood dryly.

"It looks that way," Jean admitted ruefully, feeling rather foolish at the turn of events.

"Wu Sing must have been afraid we would report to the Immigration authorities," added Louise, staring at the sign.

"Or possibly Mr. Newsome returned to make more trouble," contributed Jean. "Both Charlie Young and Wu Sing were terribly fearful of the man."

Mr. Fleetwood jotted down the address of the new laundry, but declared that he scarcely considered it worth while to go there. It was unlikely, he thought, that a countryman of Wu Sing would impart any information as to the Oriental's present whereabouts.

"I believe my time will be spent to better advantage by interviewing Mr. Wharton," declared the detective. "If you young ladies have a few more minutes to spare suppose you take me to the Beckworth Inn.''

Louise and Jean were only too glad to be of service. They accompanied the men to the hotel and arranged a meeting with the elderly gentleman, but there again disappointment awaited the detective. The old man was unable to contribute anything new to the case against David and Katherine Blore. Still weak and ill, it was a great effort for him to talk.

In a few minutes the party left the inn. Mr. Fleetwood, glancing at his watch, saw that he still had a little time before his train was due to leave.

''I should like to talk with Mrs. MacVey and look over the house,'' he told the Dana girls. ''Your information regarding a strange sleeping sickness interests me.''

''We'll be glad to take you out there,'' Louise offered instantly.

The detective and the girls went alone to the MacVey home, for Mr. Craven had a business engagement in Penfield. During the ride to the house Louise and Jean provided the detective with additional details of the baffling case, but they did not mention the little box of white powder which was in their possession, fearing that he might laugh at their theory.

Mrs. MacVey received the group cordially, inviting them into the house. At once she began a lengthy account of Donald's recent illness.

She declared that one of the other children had had a similar attack only two days previously. Jean and Louise listened for a while to the discussion, then wandered outside to play with the children.

They found the youngsters at the brook, laughing and shouting as they splashed in the shallow water. The older boys had built a small water wheel and were very proud of their achievement.

"Just look at our wheel!" Donald said proudly. "Isn't she a dandy? We built it all ourselves too!"

"I should say that is a fine wheel," Louise praised the lad, bending down to examine it. "Did you really saw the boards and nail them together all by yourselves?"

"Sure," replied Donald. "Maybe we'll build a dam next. There are just lots and lots of old boards around this place."

As the water wheel slowly turned, Louise noticed that one of the wide spokes bore printing. Curious, she stopped the revolving wheel to examine the letters. Many of them had been washed away but she could still make out certain words.

"Town of Chesterville," she read aloud. "Donald, where did you get this board?"

"Oh, I guess it came off an old box," the boy answered carelessly. "We found it in that shed over there."

As Louise straightened up, she looked at Jean. It had occurred to both girls that the printing might have a peculiar significance.

"The box may have belonged to the Blores," said Jean in a low tone.

"I was thinking the same thing."

"Possibly they received merchandise from Chesterville. While such a shipment might have no connection with the——"

"Careful," warned Louise with a quick glance which reminded her sister of the children's presence. She turned again to Donald. "You say you found this old board in the shed?"

"Yes, we keep logs there for the fireplace," answered the little boy. "Kindling wood, too."

"This board didn't come from one of your father's boxes?"

"No, it was here when we moved in."

Donald looked deeply puzzled, for he could not understand why the girls were so interested in an old board.

"Suppose we go to the shed and see if we can find the rest of the box," Louise suggested. "I have a nickel for a big red apple to the one who discovers it first."

The children ran ahead, so by the time the Dana girls reached the shed, the little folks were busy searching through the pile of wood.

"This looks like part of the box!" cried Donald, triumphantly holding up an old board.

"No, the wood is different," Jean told the boy as she examined the grain. "Anyway, the board we are after must have printing on it."

The Dana girls helped the children search but they could not find the matching piece of wood. However, as they did come upon several unmarked boards which seemed to have been part of the original box, they believed that the missing sections must have been somewhere in the shed.

"I am afraid we'll have to give up the hunt now," Louise said at last. "We've examined every board in the place."

"Not every one," replied Barbara in her piping voice. "There's a little tiny board over there in the corner. But I won't touch it 'cause it's all covered with cobwebs."

"Jean and I aren't afraid of cobwebs," laughed Louise.

She removed the piece of wood from the filmy mass which had been built around it. Carefully wiping the board with an old cloth which hung from the rafters, she suddenly gave an exclamation of pleasure.

"Jean, it has printing! And I do believe it matches the other board!"

Eagerly the girls carried the section outside into the bright sunlight. When the two boards were placed side by side, the grain of the wood matched and the lettering was of identical size and shape.

" 'Town of Chesterville,' " Jean read aloud. " '120 High Street.' "

"This address may prove of great value," Louise declared excitedly. "We must tell Mr. Fleetwood about it at once."

They gave each of the children a nickel for apples, and hastened away with their discovery. While the clue might prove to be a false one, both girls confidently believed that the Blores probably had dealings with some person in Chesterville who was connected with the smuggling case. It was reasonable to suppose that the couple had extended their operations to merchandise as well as jewels, and that they must be connected with a dishonest firm which disposed of the stolen goods for them.

Upon entering the house, the girls found Mrs. MacVey alone. "Isn't Mr. Fleetwood here?" Louise inquired, glancing about the room.

"He asked permission to look over the house. I told him he might go wherever he wished. I think you will find him on the upper floor."

The girls wandered from room to room searching for the detective. He was not upstairs. Jean called the man's name several times and was puzzled to receive no response.

"Where could he have gone?" she asked uneasily.

"I don't like this," added Louise, frowning. "So many strange things have occurred in this house that I'm almost inclined to think it *does* have a jinx on it.''

Jean gave her sister an amused glance. ''I am surprised at you, Louise. Surely you believe that everything which has happened here has a logical explanation?''

''Yes,'' agreed her sister reluctantly, ''but finding the explanation hasn't been easy. And I am worried about Mr. Fleetwood.''

''We've not searched all the downstairs rooms yet,'' Jean reminded her.

The girls went through the lower part of the house, becoming more and more alarmed. At length, reaching the den, they opened the door and glanced into the dark interior. Louise, who was slightly in advance of her sister, took a quick breath.

''Oh, I was afraid of this!'' she exclaimed fearfully.

Lying on the davenport in a sound slumber was the missing Mr. Fleetwood.

CHAPTER XXIV

THE GUARDED CLOSET

AFTER the girls had tried several times to arouse Mr. Fleetwood and had failed, they were certain that he had become a victim of the strange sleep which had fallen upon so many persons in the old Wharton house. Louise called Mrs. MacVey. With her assistance the three carried the detective to a first floor bedroom and made him comfortable.

"He should come out of the sleep in a few hours," Jean declared reassuringly.

"Even so, I shall not stay in this house another day unless the mystery is cleared up," declared Mrs. MacVey excitedly. "Why, this makes five persons who have been stricken here —Mr. Wharton, Louise, Mr. Fleetwood, and the two children."

"I don't blame you at all," returned Louise gravely. "The mystery *must* be solved."

"But how?"

"Jean and I have a clue," replied the girl, glancing at the board which she had carried into the house. "A clue which leads to Chesterville."

"Chesterville?" inquired Mrs. MacVey in a puzzled tone. "Where is that?"

"About ten miles southeast of Penfield. Jean, let's take Mr. Fleetwood's taxicab and try to find High Street."

"How much money have you in your purse?"

"Enough to pay the fare, I think," replied Louise.

"I can lend you some money," Mrs. MacVey offered quickly. "If you really have a clue which will solve this baffling case, I urge you to trace it down before any other accidents occur."

"What about school?" Jean asked her sister dubiously. "We can't try Mrs. Crandall's patience too far!"

"We'll explain to our headmistress later. If we are successful, she'll excuse us, I am sure. This is very important."

"If the trip turns out to be a wild chase, we'll probably have our social privileges curtailed for the remainder of the term! Let's take a chance anyway."

Without explaining the nature of their clue to Mrs. MacVey, the Danas hastened to the waiting cab and ordered the driver to go at once to Chesterville. Arriving some time later at the town they toured the outlying section in search of 120 High Street. Presently Jean caught sight of the number on a dingy looking frame building sadly in need of paint.

Telling the driver to stop a little way up the

street, Louise and Jean walked back to the house. There was no sign of anyone about the premises, and their knock was not answered.

"The place looks deserted to me," Louise declared in disappointment.

Jean had turned away and was glancing up the street toward an approaching automobile.

"Louise!" she exclaimed, pulling her sister behind a clump of bushes. "That looks like Ed Newsome's car."

"It is, Jean! And Katherine and David Blore are with him! Oh, what luck!"

Crouched low behind the bushes, the girls waited. In a moment the automobile drew up at the curb. The three friends alighted.

"You folks go on in," the man told the Blores. "I'll bring the suitcases."

Katherine and her brother unlocked the front door and went into the house. However, thinking that Ed Newsome might have trouble in handling so many bags, they both returned a moment later to help him.

"Now is our chance," whispered Jean tensely. "Let's steal into the house while their backs are turned."

"It's dangerous, Jean."

"Yes, but we'll never learn anything out here," her daring sister reminded her.

Watching for an opportunity, the girls quietly slipped into the house without being observed. They found themselves in a living room which was furnished almost entirely with Oriental furniture and luxurious scatter rugs from the Asiatic countries.

"I'll venture to guess Newsome forced wealthy Chinese persons to contribute all these things," Jean whispered as the girls gazed about in awe. "Either that or he obtained them from his many smuggling activities."

The only possible hiding place was provided by a large, carved imported screen in one corner of the room. Scarcely had the sisters secreted themselves behind it when Newsome and his companions entered the house with their luggage.

"Did you get the tickets for South America, Dave?" the other man inquired as he closed the door.

"Yes," replied Blore briefly. "No questions asked, either."

"Good! We'll get off on that steamer to-night. Once we're safely out of the country, the police will forget about the case."

"We're not safely away yet," observed Katherine Blore uneasily. "I don't like the way the police are closing in on us."

"Now don't start worrying again," Newsome retorted impatiently. "Gather up all the things worth taking and pack your clothes. We'll be away from here in half an hour."

To the disappointment of Louise and Jean the three carried their suitcases upstairs. All they could hear of the conversation was an indistinct mumble of voices.

"We *must* find out more," Louise whispered tensely.

The Danas tiptoed up the stairway. Just as Jean in the lead reached the last step it creaked beneath her weight.

"What was that?" asked Miss Blore sharply.

"Nothing," answered her brother impatiently. "You're getting so you are afraid of your own shadow."

"I am nervous," the woman admitted.

The girls slipped quietly into a vacant bedroom. They pressed their ears against the wall and listened.

"I learned today that a family by the name of MacVey has taken the old Wharton house," Ed Newsome remarked to his companions.

"That so?" inquired David Blore. "Well, I guess the stuff we left there will be safe until we get back from South America."

"You should have destroyed the crown from which the jewels were taken," Newsome declared, a note of worry in his voice. "If it were found it would serve as damaging evidence against us."

"It won't be found, Ed," David Blore said confidently. "By the way, that crown is pure gold, and we can have it melted down later."

"The MacVeys may discover it while we are in South America."

"If they do, they'll remember nothing about it," Miss Blore said significantly.

"What do you mean?"

"David and I hid the crown in a secret closet. It is safeguarded by a powder which has the power to produce deep sleep. Whenever the closet door is opened, the intruder takes a breath and off to sleep he goes. Awakening, he remembers nothing of what has happened."

"Clever, eh?" demanded David Blore proudly. "I had a chemist make up the powder according to my own formula."

"My good friends, I see I have underrated you both," replied Newsome flatteringly. "I shall borrow some of that powder from you. It might be useful in covering our escape if the authorities should press us too closely."

"Unfortunately we haven't any with us," answered Katherine Blore. "We left the ranch in such a hurry we forgot to pack our supply of powder."

Jean and Louise had heard every word of the conversation with fast beating hearts. Katherine Blore's admission definitely cleared up the mystery of why so many persons had fallen asleep at the old Wharton house! In turn Louise, Mr. Wharton, Mr. Fleetwood, and the MacVey children had discovered the secret closet, only to breathe the fumes from the powder, fall into slumber, and recall nothing later.

The woman's remark regarding the hasty

departure from the Bar II ranch brought to mind the little black box which the Dana girls had found in the study of old Mrs. Blore's home. At that very moment Louise had the container in her handbag.

She tried to signal this fact to Jean. Failing to make her sister understand, she unfastened the bag and took out the little black box. Jean grinned appreciatively. Then the smile faded from her face, for with no warning the bedroom door opened. Ed Newsome entered, stopping short as he saw the girls.

"Dave!" he shouted. "Come here, quick!"

Louise and Jean made a wild dash for the hallway, but their escape was cut off by David and Katherine Blore.

"Oh, no you don't!" cried the man jeeringly. "You'll not tell what you have overheard to the police!"

"Grab them!" urged David Blore, leaping toward Louise.

The girl eluded his grasp and backed toward the wall. A desperate plan of escape for the Danas and capture for the others took form in her mind.

"Keep away," she warned. "If you don't——"

The man laughed as he came steadily toward her. Turning her own face away so that she would not breathe the fumes, Louise unfastened the lid of the little black box. As David Blore bore down upon her, she hurled the powder. Some of it went squarely into the man's face, the remainder fell on the floor close to where the man's sister and Newsome were struggling to overpower Jean.

The Blores did not notice the black box nor seem to realize the nature of the powder. After the first moment of hope Louise began to think that she had overestimated the power of the white dust. Seemingly it had no effect upon anyone in the room.

"I'll teach you not to try any more of your tricks, young lady!" exclaimed David Blore cruelly.

With an ugly laugh he seized the girl's arm and twisted it painfully!

CHAPTER XXV

A Signed Confession

LOUISE abandoned all hope. Although she struggled violently, she knew she must submit to capture. Then unexpectedly Blore's grip relaxed on her arm. Reaching a hand to his throat, he began to gasp for breath. Slowly he sagged to the floor.

Louise felt her own strength failing. The powder was producing its effect on her, too! She reeled backwards into the hallway.

Across the room Miss Blore and Newsome had turned to stare in amazement at the woman's brother. Before they understood what had happened to him, they too began to feel the effects of the powder.

As their fingers became powerless, **Jean** slipped from her captor's grasp. When the couple slumped to the floor, she held her breath and rushed to the door, collapsing in Louise's arms.

Together the Danas half tumbled down the stairway to the front door. The fresh air revived them but it was a long while before either could speak.

"That—was a—close call," Jean murmured

at last. "Another whiff of those fumes—and we would have—gone under, too!"

"Newsome and the Blores should sleep for hours," Louise said after a moment. "We must call the police at once."

Their taxi driver, tired of waiting so long, had departed. Still feeling weak and light-headed, the girls got to the nearest police station as fast as they could. They had great difficulty in making the captain believe their story, but at last he sent a squad of policemen to the house with the girls. One glance at the three persons lying asleep on the floor was enough to convince them. Terse orders were given that the victims be taken in the patrol wagon to the precinct.

"You've done a fine job," the captain praised the girls when they returned. "This man Newsome is a notorious crook, the head of a gang of smugglers. He uses several aliases and for years has eluded the authorities, living in the height of luxury."

"And the Blores?" inquired Louise as the unconscious brother and sister were carried to cells.

"We know less about them," the man replied. "Apparently they are agents for Newsome, fairly new to the smuggling ring."

"Jean and I may be able to contribute a little evidence," replied Louise quietly. "We over-heard their conversation with Mr. Newsome."

She then told the police officer that the couple had admitted their part in the theft of the crown jewels.

"Did they say where the jewels had been hidden?" the officer questioned tersely.

Louise shook her head. "No, we didn't learn that part."

"Probably somewhere in the house at 120 High. We'll search the place from top to bottom. By the way, how did you knock out the prisoners so effectively? You didn't use chloroform?"

"Oh, no," replied Jean innocently.

She and Louise quickly made an excuse for leaving and did not reveal their secret. They also had withheld from the officers their information that the missing crown had been hidden in a secret closet at the MacVey home, wishing to have the thrill of discovering it for themselves.

"Let's go back there right away," Jean proposed eagerly.

Taking another cab, they soon reached the place. Mr. Fleetwood was sleeping still. This suited the girls' purpose very well. Telling Mrs. MacVey that they wished to do a bit of exploring, they equipped themselves with face masks made from damp towels and roamed about the house searching for the sinister closet.

"Be careful if you come upon anything which appears to be a secret panel," Louise warned her sister.

After spending half an hour in futile search, the girls were very discouraged.

"Somehow I have a feeling the hiding place may be in the den," Louise said thoughtfully. "Let's concentrate our efforts there."

Going to the lower floor room, they made a thorough inspection. Next to the den they found a large closet which Mrs. MacVey was using for the storage of suitcases and trunks. Apparently it had not been cleaned since the family had moved in, for the walls were covered with dust. Jean brushed some of it away. Suddenly she gave a cry of pleasure.

"Louise, I see a faint outline on the wall! I think I have found the secret panel!"

Before Louise could advise her sister to use caution, Jean groped her hand over the wall. As she touched a hidden spring, the panel moved sideways, revealing a large opening.

"I've found it!" cried Jean. In her great excitement the girl did not notice that the towel had slipped from her face.

"Your mask!" warned Louise frantically. "Pull it up!"

Jean quickly pulled the cover over her nose and mouth again. Feeling a trifle light-headed, she sat down in a chair for an instant, while Louise reached her hand into the opening and drew forth the golden crown. Then she quickly closed the panel so that fumes from the powder within would not escape into the room.

In a moment the girls opened the windows and removed their masks. Triumphantly they examined the treasure.

"This crown will serve as damaging evidence against Newsome and the Blores!" declared Louise. "Oh, Jean, I believe we've practically solved the case. Isn't it wonderful!"

"Won't Mr. Fleetwood be surprised when he wakes up!"

Considerable time had elapsed since the detective's collapse. A little later when the girls carried their treasure to the bedroom, they found that he had aroused. Both he and Mrs. MacVey listened incredulously as Louise and Jean offered a complete account of their recent adventure.

"I couldn't believe it if you didn't have the crown to prove your words," Mr. Fleetwood declared, shaking his head. "And to think I slept through everything! I have half a mind to turn in my badge—and ask that similar ones be given to you girls!"

Later he accompanied the Danas to the police station where they delivered the crown into the hands of the authorities. Learning that the missing jewels had not been found yet, Jean and Louise provided the officers with a copy of the list they had discovered in the cobweb at the Blore ranch.

They were present when Ed Newsome was questioned again. Convinced that he could not escape prison, and hoping to receive a lighter sentence, the man finally revealed that the stolen gems were hidden under a floor in the house on High Street.

The jewels were recovered soon by the police. With the assistance of Mr. Fleetwood and Mr. Craven, the Dana girls checked the cache with their own original list, and were satisfied that all the gems had been found.

Confronted with Newsome's confession, Katherine Blore bitterly denounced her associate and admitted her own part in the smuggling plot. She signed a statement to the effect that she had stolen the crown jewels from the museum, arranging everything to give the appearance that she had fallen overboard from the *Balaska.*

Actually she had dressed as a steward and had hidden in the hold of the vessel, keeping the stolen gems with her. When an opportunity came she slipped ashore without being observed. Captain Dana's subsequent investigation had compelled her to flee with her brother to the western ranch where their mother lived.

"And just think," declared Jean, when the confession was read to her, "if Frances Roy hadn't invited Louise and me to New Mexico, the mystery never might have been solved!"

After receiving the congratulations of the police officers, the Dana girls hastened to a telegraph station, from which they sent a long mes-

sage to Captain Dana, telling him that Miss
Blore was under arrest and had admitted her
guilt.

"This will be a big load off Uncle Ned's
mind," Jean said with a happy sigh as she and
Louise boarded a bus for Starhurst School.
"His troubles are over now."

"And ours are just beginning. Do you realize what time it is?"

"I haven't the slightest idea."

"Four o'clock."

"And we've had no lunch!"

"Lunch!" exclaimed Louise. "I never even
thought about that. Anyway, we have more serious concerns. Mrs. Crandall will be waiting
for us."

"Even if she takes away all our privileges
for a year, the day was worth it," laughed Jean
happily.

"Yes, it was," agreed Louise with deep con-
tentment. "I never hope to have such a thrilling time again in all my life."

Lettie Briggs was the first person to accost
the Dana girls when they reached the school.
Evidently she had been awaiting them.

"You'll catch it now," she said with a spiteful smile. "Mrs. Crandall says you are to come
straight to her office."

"We were going there anyway," replied
Jean, not in the least disturbed by the order.

The Dana girls spent half an hour with the

headmistress. When they finally left the office, Lettie was loitering nearby. She was disappointed to observe that Louise and Jean did not appear in the least crestfallen. Instead both were smiling and appeared to be in high spirits. They went directly to the kitchen, where, apparently by Mrs. Crandall's order, they were given a special meal.

"Favoritism," Lettie reported angrily to Ina Mason. "It's just no use trying to combat it."

Within a few days everyone in the school learned the details of the Dana girls' adventure. For a week it was the main topic of conversation. Louise and Jean were urged to tell the same story over so many times that at last they rebelled.

No one was more delighted at the outcome than Frances Roy. She wrote a letter to her parents telling them of the honors which had fallen upon her friends. Her mother wrote back, congratulating Louise and Jean, and she added the news that old Mrs. Blore had died soon after their departure for the East.

"If the poor old lady had to go, perhaps it is better that she died without learning her adopted children will be sent to prison," Louise commented sadly.

In the days which followed, Mr. Fleetwood and the immigration authorities made many attempts to trace Charlie Young and Wu Sing. They were never found, and the Dana girls could not feel sorry, for the two men had aided them materially in establishing a case against Ed Newsome.

Soon after the three smugglers had been sentenced to prison, Jean received word that the government would grant a patent for her music-recording machine. Then indeed, Lettie Briggs' dissatisfaction reached its highest peak. For days she went about in gloom, refusing to speak to the other students or take part in special school activities.

The Danas paid little attention to the spoiled girl, who never learned to profit from experience. She was to bother Jean and Louise much in their next case, "The Secret at the Gatehouse." Just now they thought it best to forget her and enjoy the solution of their recent mystery.

In due time a letter came from Captain Dana adding his praise to the congratulations already showered upon the girls. Aunt Harriet wrote also, sending them a large box of homemade cookies, cake and other sweets for a special party. Louise and Jean promptly invited all their friends to share an evening feast.

"This is really a double victory celebration," declared Evelyn Starr gaily, as the girls sat in a circle about the spread.

"What do you mean?" inquired Jean dubiously. "I thought we were here just to eat a lot of Aunt Harriet's good food."

"Oh, no, the occasion has far more importance than that," corrected Evelyn, and the other girls nodded agreement. "We are celebrating the successful culmination of the crown jewel mystery and Jean's debut as an inventor!"

The girls raised their cups of steaming chocolate; and when Jean said gaily, "Let's drink to the next mystery Louise and I will solve," she never dreamed she was proposing a toast to "The Secret at the Gatehouse."